I0544088

DANIA VOSS

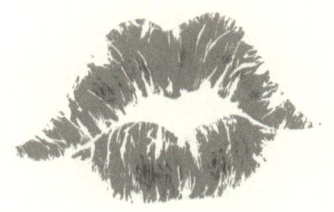

EVERNIGHT PUBLISHING ®

www.evernightpublishing.com

Copyright© 2018

Dania Voss

Editor: Karyn White

Cover Artist: Jay Aheer

ISBN: 978-1-77339-794-8

ALL RIGHTS RESERVED

WARNING: The unauthorized reproduction or distribution of this copyrighted work is illegal. No part of this book may be used or reproduced electronically or in print without written permission, except in the case of brief quotations embodied in reviews.

This is a work of fiction. All names, characters, and places are fictitious. Any resemblance to actual events, locales, organizations, or persons, living or dead, is entirely coincidental.

DANIA VOSS

DEDICATION

Many thanks to Stacey and everyone at Evernight Publishing. You have been a joy to work with. I would also like to acknowledge the Evernight author community as a whole—you are an amazing group of talented, supportive, and crazy fun people. I've truly enjoyed getting to know you over the last several months. I am honored to be a part of this family.

To all the men and women in uniform past, present, and future as well as their families—thank you for your service and sacrifice.

DANIA VOSS

THE WARRIOR'S WHISPER

Windy City Nights, 1

Dania Voss

Copyright © 2018

Chapter One

Feeling smothered and struggling to breathe, Heath Jackson bolted upright, damp with sweat and chilled. It was still dark. He scrambled, reaching over to his left in desperate search of his small tactical knife and fell, hitting the ground with a thud.

He needed to assess the situation immediately, or lives would be lost, but he was disoriented and his head felt heavy. He shook it, needing his brain to stop rattling in around in his skull and swiped angrily at the tears streaming down his face.

He didn't have time for this shit; he needed his weapon. Needed to act. Now. His Marine unit was depending on him. Some of his unit brothers were just kids at only nineteen and twenty years old, and Taliban insurgents and IEDs, improvised explosive devices, were everywhere.

Fumbling around on the ground frantically looking for his knife and breathing in as much air as he could, he was confused. What kind of terrain was this? It wasn't sand. Or dirt. *What the hell?*

As light streamed into view he panicked. Where was his knife? He needed his damn knife! Someone was calling his name, but the sound was cut off, significantly muted and difficult to make out.

"Heath! Heath!"

He looked up toward the door, breathing heavily, heart racing. He clenched his fists, since he didn't have his knife, ready to attack.

A figure loomed in the doorway, wearing boxers. The man looked familiar, but he didn't think he should be in Sangin, Afghanistan. He was fairly certain he wasn't military.

"It's Jake! It's Jake!"

Heath pressed his hands against his head, willing it to feel right again. Jake? He knew that name. Where did he know that name from?

"Heath! It's Jake! It's Jake! Your best friend Jake!"

"Jake? What are you doing here? I can't find my knife! I can't protect you! The Taliban!" Why were sounds so damned muted? He needed to protect his friend. Jake. He'd known Jake since they were little boys. And he wasn't a soldier. Hadn't been trained. Heath needed to protect him or he'd die. He couldn't lose another friend on the battlefield.

"You're home! You're safe! You're home! There's no Taliban! Just us! We're safe! We're safe!"

Home? Heath felt around the ground again. Not sand or dirt. Carpeting. He was touching carpeting. He pulled in a few more deep breaths, glancing around, slowly reorienting himself. His bedroom. He was in his bedroom, not Sangin, Afghanistan. He'd had another combat nightmare. And today of all days. *Shit.*

What was Jake doing gesturing with his hands

like that and pointing?

"Put your hearing aids in!"

Heath's stomach sank. Sign language. Jake was signing. Why? Because he'd lost about seventy percent of his hearing on October 13[th,] 2010, because of all those fucking IEDs. So many IEDs, every-fucking-where. His family and close friends had learned how to sign—because of him. *Damn it.*

He turned to his nightstand where his hearing aids and knife sat, exactly where he'd placed them the night before. He slipped his hearing aids in and grabbed his knife, the cool metal in his hand comforting him. Jake cautiously stepped further into the room but didn't crowd him, knowing Heath didn't like to be touched after a combat nightmare.

"You with me, buddy?" Jake asked tentatively.

Heath blew out a breath and got up off the floor and sat on the edge of his bed. He nodded, embarrassed Jake had to see him at his worst. Normally when he woke up from a nightmare, he was alone. Always alone. Even with Jake but a few feet away, he still felt that way.

He gripped his knife so hard his skin turned white. "I should check—"

Jake held up a hand. "I already checked the house. We're alone. The alarm is still engaged. None of the entry points have been breached. We're good."

That provided Heath with some level of comfort. But he felt like an idiot. "I'm sorry I woke you. This is an important day, and I've already ruined it."

Jake scoffed, shaking his head. "You didn't ruin anything. I was already up. I'm kind of wound up, you know?" Jake's smile lit up his face, and he couldn't help but smile back.

Heath stood and went to his friend. A man he considered a little brother after decades of friendship. He hugged Jake tight, finally feeling more like himself. When Jake hugged him back, he laughed.

"Of course I know. My little brother's getting married today. You've earned the right to be wound up," Heath said as he ended their embrace.

"Hell, yeah. I know it's all supposed to be about the bride today, but I'm psyched. If you're … all right, I'm going to shower up and see about some breakfast." Jake's hopeful expression made him feel like a fool. It was his friend's wedding day, and he was worried about his mental state. Heath was supposed to be helping *him* today, not the other way around.

"I'm going to be fine. Don't worry about me. I'll get ready and help with breakfast."

Jake nodded and left his room, whistling happily as he went. When he heard Jake close the hallway bathroom door, Heath grabbed his cell phone from the nightstand and speed dialed the only person nearby who understood what he'd gone through because he'd been with him when it had all gone to shit.

"Hey, brother." Rocco Moretti, former Marine Gunnery Sergeant, answered on the second ring.

"I had another one, today of all fucking days." He sighed and sat on the edge of the bed. "Are they ever going to stop?"

Rocco grunted. Heath had met the Italian-American when Rocco's unit had joined Heath's in Sangin three weeks before Heath was injured. After discovering they were both from the Chicagoland area with Heath from Elmhurst and Rocco's family from nearby Lombard and Villa Park, they'd become fast friends. They'd stayed close even after being discharged a short time after the battle that had taken much of Heath's hearing and ended his military career.

"I doubt it, but I hope over time we'll have fewer

of them," Rocco offered.

Heath closed his eyes and rolled his shoulders. "Just once, I'd like for the dream to end without seeing Jones, Williams, and Coleman blown to shit right in front of us."

Rocco sighed over the line. "Your mind's not going to let you rewrite history, brother."

He knew Rocco was right, but he still wished things were different. He despised the feeling of helplessness that came over him at times for not being able to save his fallen brothers.

"Need me to come over?"

Heath stood and stretched. He'd be all right. He had to be. He needed to be at his best for Jake today and the entire weekend.

"No, I'm all right. Jake was already up. He's taking a shower, and then we're making breakfast." His stomach growled as if on cue.

"My brother emailed me some research he did on what he says are effective non-medical PTSD treatments. I haven't really gone over it yet, but I'll email it to you."

He knew Rocco's younger brother Massimo meant well. He was a good guy and just wanted to help. Were these treatments actually effective though? Who knew? "Sure, thanks."

"Good. I'll see you later at church. And no Catholic jokes. I'll be fine in a Lutheran church," he warned.

Heath couldn't help himself. He had to ask. "So, who are you wearing today? Gucci, Prada, Dolce & Gabbana?" He chuckled when Rocco didn't answer right away. Women swooned over the olive-skinned, brown-eyed man, especially when he dressed to the nines in an Italian designer suit, silk tie, and leather shoes. And when he spoke in his family's native tongue, you'd think he'd just arrived from Catania, Sicily where the Moretti side of the family was from.

"*Stronzo*."

He full out laughed, fairly certain *stronzo* wasn't an Italian designer. More than likely a curse word. "I've never heard of that label. Are they a new Italian designer? Someone I should know about?"

"*Stronzo* means asshole, you asshole. And you fucking know my cousins get my suits, ties, and shoes at a big discount. It wouldn't hurt for *you* to step up *your* game every once in a while, *brother*."

Still laughing, Heath made one last dig. "I'll keep that in mind, *brother*. You still haven't answered the question though."

"Armani," Rocco replied with a smile in his voice and disconnected the call.

Feeling a little lighter emotionally, Heath tossed his phone back on the nightstand and tugged on a pair of track pants. On the first floor of his townhouse he found Jake in a t-shirt and jeans working on breakfast. Orange juice had been poured and sausage links were sizzling in a skillet. From the looks of it Jake had settled on ham and cheese omelets for breakfast on his wedding day. That worked for Heath.

"What can I do to help?" he asked not wanting to leave all the work to the groom.

"Everything's just about ready. Go ahead and toast up the bread. White for me."

With multi-grain and white toast ready, preserves and butter laid out, Heath waited in his chair for Jake to bring everything he'd prepared to the table. It smelled delicious. He was starving and ready to for a more positive, upbeat rest of the day.

Today was a day for celebration, love, and family. Good food, good drink, and dancing. Not for nightmares.

They dug into their breakfasts with gusto. Heath was happy for Jake. His fiancée, Cassie, was a wonderful woman. And one who had endured a long courtship until Jake felt he could support them on his salary alone if she wanted to stay home after they started a family.

"Look, Jake, I'm sorry—" Heath began before Jake put his hand up to stop him.

"Don't, okay? There's no reason to apologize. I'm sorry you still get those nightmares. I just wish there was something I could do to help." Jake continued eating his breakfast.

Heath nodded and followed suit. He wished something could be done, too. Sleeping pills, even at their lowest dosage, left him too out of it in the morning, although usually nightmare-free. He needed to be sharp at the office, especially now. He'd figure something out. At least he hoped he would. Nightmares were only a part of his struggles since being discharged. Maybe some of the PTSD treatments Rocco's brother researched would offer some relief.

Jake finished off his orange juice and regarded him seriously. *Uh oh.*

"You know, it's about time *you* settled down, don't you think? I mean, you're not getting any younger."

Heath snorted. "Why is it every time someone gets married, they want everyone around them to get paired up?" He was only thirty-five, not an old man by any means. It wasn't his age that prevented Heath from settling down.

No. There were his issues since being discharged, which were no laughing matter and a lot to ask any woman to deal with. It was that and the fact the only woman who he'd ever consider being serious with, couldn't and wouldn't ever be his. Jake, even though he didn't know it, was one of the reasons why.

"Because we want everyone to be as happy as we are. To have someone who loves them to come home to, share their life with, build a family with. Grow old together. Don't you want that? Maybe a couple mini-Heaths running around?" Jake stood from the table, rinsed his plate, the pans he'd used, the serving dishes and loaded them into the dishwasher. He leaned against the counter and studied him intently.

Heath wanted all those things. He just didn't believe he'd ever get them, especially not now after going through hell in Afghanistan. The shit, as his military brothers referred to it. It wasn't easy to explain it to a civilian who hadn't lived through it. And he certainly wouldn't share the gruesome details of his time in the Marines with his friend on his wedding day.

"Yes, I have thought about it. Of course. But wives don't just fall out of the sky, you know? And right now, I'm not in the best frame of mind for a serious relationship." *And the woman I want is off limits because she's your little sister Leah and she works for me, too.*

Jake smiled, seeming to contemplate what he'd just said. He didn't look convinced though. "Maybe. But you never know. There'll be a lot of single ladies at the wedding, and you never know what could happen," he said, waggling his eyebrows.

"Really? You're pushing wedding hookups now?" Heath stood, nudged Jake away from the sink, rinsed his breakfast plate and added it to the other dishes in the dishwasher.

Jake shrugged, still smiling like an idiot. "You never know. Sometimes hookups, at a wedding or somewhere else, can become something more. Keep an open mind, that's all I'm saying."

Heath chuckled at Jake's enthusiasm and optimism. "I will. You have my word."

"Great. I'm going to see what's on. We still have a few hours before we need to head to the church." Jake left the room, leaving Heath alone with his thoughts.

A wedding hookup? There was no harm in it, he supposed. It would be a great way to end a day that began like shit. Balls deep in some pretty girl after all the wedding festivities were over. He could think of worse ways to end the day. The only problem was— he wanted to hookup with Leah. *I want more than just a hookup.*

"Never going to happen, pal," he mumbled to himself. He set off for his en-suite bathroom upstairs while Jake was busy flipping through channels on his big screen TV in the living room.

He stripped down in the bathroom and shaved before stepping under the hot shower spray. Heath was anxious to wash away the ugly start to the morning and move on. He was determined to be upbeat and enthusiastic, like Jake. For Jake. He deserved that from him, and he'd get it.

As he washed his hair he thought about what Jake had said about hooking up tonight. Not a bad idea, but when his thoughts wandered to Leah as they often did, he got hard. He'd jerked off to visions of the dark-haired, curvy beauty countless times. Every time he felt like he was betraying his friend, and every time he felt guilty because she was ten years his junior. He'd known her since the day she was born and had regarded her more like a younger sister than anything else.

Until she'd grown up.

Adjusting the shower temperature to cold, he willed his erection away. No way in hell would he stroke his dick to thoughts of Leah with her brother nearby. He wasn't *that* much of an asshole.

Once he was dressed in a t-shirt and jeans and ready to go, he grabbed the garment bag with his black tails and went back downstairs to join Jake. He found him on the couch watching *27 Dresses*. He tossed the garment bag on the loveseat and shook his head, sitting down beside Jake on the couch.

"Really, man?"

Jake shrugged, not seeming bothered. "Not much else was on and I'm getting married today. Just keeping things light."

Heath was on board with keeping things light after the disaster from earlier this morning. They watched the movie and bullshitted around until their ride to church arrived.

It was a perfect day for a wedding he thought, as they stepped outside to their waiting black stretch limousine. He lifted his face to the sky, enjoying the warm June sun shining down on him. After a couple deep breaths, he felt recharged and energized. It was going to be a great day, he'd make sure of it.

Jake shook his head, glancing at the open limo car door, the dark-suited driver standing beside it waiting on them to get inside. "Luke went all out, huh," he said as he got inside.

Heath followed him in, and the door thunked closed. "Come on. It's your wedding day. Give him a break."

He and Jake settled in for the short ride to Grace of God Lutheran Church on Kenilworth. "You ever think when Luke's family moved into the house between ours he'd become the star pitcher for the Chicago Cobras, one of the best pitchers in the majors, and a celebrity on top of it?" Jake asked as he glanced out the window.

He scoffed and shook his head. "How could I? He was only two years old when we met him. All I thought at the time was he had such golden blond hair and the cutest dimples I'd ever seen at the age of seven. You were only four yourself."

Christ. Luke was thirty now. He'd known him and Jake for nearly three decades. Maybe Jake was right. He wasn't getting any younger and seriously needed to think about the future. He wished things weren't fucked up in so many ways. It would make everything a lot easier.

"Yeah, I know. And the Stryker family was so down to earth, considering they owned the team and so much real estate in Chicago and the nearby suburbs."

Heath was a "money guy" but didn't make a habit of trying to figure out his friend's net worth, although he had a fairly good idea. Luke was closing in on billionaire status before he even assumed ownership of the team when he retired from baseball in the next couple of years.

Jake was out of the limo just as it came to a stop in front of Grace of God. The man was excited, that was for certain. Heath didn't blame him one bit. He hurried to catch up with him inside and came to a stop right behind him mid-way up the aisle. The inside of the church was barren. *Shit.*

"Hello, guys!" a dark-haired man wearing a grey skinny suit chirped as he stepped into the church from a side door. Why was he so chipper when the church wasn't ready yet?

Heath sidestepped Jake and got in the man's face. "What's going on? Where are the flowers? If you fu— flub this up for Jake and Cassie we're going to have a big problem. This is unacceptable." If they weren't in a church he'd rip this guy a new asshole.

The jerk just smiled and glanced over to Jake. "This must be Heath, the Marine?"

Screw this, he didn't care they were in a church.

"What difference does being a Marine make? We're talking about flowers. *Missing* flowers and whatever else Cassie and Jake wanted for the ceremony."

Jake placed a comforting hand on his shoulder. He knew Jake had to be upset. They had a plan for today, and Chicago's premiere event planners Hailey's Events was doing a shit job.

"Let Joe explain what's going on. I'm sure everything's fine, right, Joe?" Jake didn't sound so sure. He just *hoped* everything was fine.

Joe, AKA skinny suit jerk, took a deep breath and nodded. "First off, thank you for your service, Heath."

Heath sighed. He didn't need to be thanked. People thought they were being thoughtful and patriotic when they said that. Truth was, they'd never know what it was like to serve, especially in combat. What active military, veterans, and their families needed were programs and support for their physical and psychological injuries, housing and job programs. Assistance for their homeless.

He nodded, not wanting to get into it. The man was trying to be nice. It wasn't *his* fault service members, veterans, and their families needed much more than kind words.

"I know emotions are high, but trust me. We are the best in the business. You're both a little early. The florists are on their way, due in the next few minutes. Hannah, the owner's daughter, is finishing up in Fellowship Hall setting up refreshments your guests will enjoy after the ceremony. I assure you both, everything will be *exactly* the way you planned it *and* on schedule."

"Thank you," he and Jake said in unison. It would be all right.

"Why don't I show you to the room where you'll get dressed?" Joe offered, still upbeat and friendly.

Heath handed Jake his garment bag. He needed a moment. "Can you take this for me? I'm going to sit a minute, if that's all right."

Jake took his garment bag with an understanding smile on his face. "No problem, man. I'll be back in a few."

He sat down in one of the pews to his left and leaned back, looking up. The church's entire domed ceiling was painted with various biblical scenes. Whoever conceived of this vision for the ceiling was a true artist. The artwork was awe-inspiring, spiritual, and calming.

Still leaning back, he closed his eyes, allowing the church's soothing calm to wash over him. He slowly breathed in and out, each breath settling him down closer to where to he needed to be.

Lord, care for the souls of the fallen who fought bravely but paid the ultimate price for our freedom. Bless the families and loved ones they left behind. Continue to watch over those currently serving and those who will serve in the future. I ask and pray for everlasting peace. One life lost is one too many. Thank you for your continued blessings and for bringing Cassie to Jake. Bless their marriage and future family.

Before he could finish, he sensed Jake just as he sat down beside him. It would be all right. He'd have more time before they went to the reception later.

"I just got a text from Rocco. He's on point for Dixon-Shaw for Luke's security today. They'll be here soon," Jake informed him happily.

That made sense since he and Luke had become close friends. Jake, too, for that matter. Heath and Rocco had reconnected after they were discharged from the Marines and his brood had welcomed and accepted the Italian as a member of their family.

Suddenly the church was bustling with floral workers carrying various tools of their trade, white and cornflower blue ribbons—and flowers, so many flowers.

"See? Told you they'd be here on time," Heath teased Jake and stood up. They needed to clear out and get out of the way.

Jake chuckled, shaking his head. "Yeah, you told me so. Just before you almost ripped poor Joe's head off."

Heath got irritated more easily now since getting injured and could overreact at times. "Well—I *probably* wouldn't have hurt him," he said, trying to make light of his behavior earlier. "But you have to admit, you were a little nervous when we walked in and you saw how bare the church was."

Jake shrugged. "I was, I won't deny it. But I would have waited for Joe to explain before blowing a gasket. Just saying."

Of course Jake was right. Heath knew that. But he couldn't do anything about it right now. He'd apologize to Joe later. It was the least he could do.

Jake stood and snapped a few pictures of the organized chaos on his cell phone before leading them through various corridors toward the back of the church to the room where they'd get dressed.

Heath was ready to get the show on the road. Support one of his closest friends on his wedding day. Eat, drink, and be merry. And if he played his cards right, a wedding night hookup. He tried to ignore the knot in his stomach at the thought of Leah hooking up tonight with some random wedding guest. But what could he do? He had no claim over her and never would.

Jake led them through a room doorway, and he welcomed the sight of Luke placing his garment bag on a table next to theirs. The pitcher's million-dollar dimpled smile always felt like old times.

"There he is! Mr. Big Time professional athlete." The gang was back together. It was exactly what Heath's soul needed.

"Well, you know me. Places to go, people to see," Luke teased back.

Jake hugged Luke tight, seemingly overcome with emotion. "It's good to see you, man. I'm so glad you're here."

"I wouldn't miss today for the world, even though I couldn't be here for the rehearsal."

Heath waited for the groom to finish greeting Luke, anxious for a minute with the man himself. It was Jake's day, and he wouldn't stand in the way.

"So, I hear you're gracing us with your presence through the weekend," Heath joked. There would be plenty of time to catch up.

"You heard right, big brother. Don't *you* feel lucky," Luke kidded back.

Jake ended their embrace and clapped Luke on the back near his shoulder. Not hard in Heath's opinion, but the star pitcher visibly winced. *Damn it.* Something was wrong with his pitching arm.

• Chapter Two

Leah waited impatiently in the vestibule of Grace of God Lutheran Church for her older brother Jake's wedding ceremony to begin. After seven long years, he was marrying Cassie Jayne and had a baby on the way. That little tidbit of information was supposed to remain a secret until Cassie passed her first trimester.

She hoped Jake realized what a lucky man he was. How many women as amazing as Cassie would wait that long to get married? Not many, that was for damn sure.

You would. You've waited all your life for Heath, and you're still *waiting.*

She sighed and shook her head. Pathetic, that's what she was. Waiting on a man who saw her as nothing but his friend's little sister and his employee.

Even though she was Jake's younger sister, she was not a little girl. Not anymore. She was a twenty-five-year-old woman, a Northwestern University graduate with a finance degree, a kick-ass financial analyst for the Chicago Cobras and a pretty amazing chick if she did say so herself.

If Heath hadn't known her since the day she was born, she knew in her heart and soul he would see her as a woman. A woman that belonged to him. Always had and always would. As pathetic as she felt waiting for Jake's wedding ceremony to begin, she knew without a doubt Heath had ruined her for every other man even though they'd never been together romantically.

How sad was that? Heath still called her "little girl" away from the office, like he did when she was. That needed to stop.

She had selected her white lacey lingerie and

matching white lace-topped thigh-highs with care and purpose. Her high heels completed her look. At only five feet five her heels gave her a little extra height to Heath's six feet three sexy, muscular, tattooed frame.

She wasn't sure how yet, but Leah's intention was for Heath to get more than a peek at what was under her bridesmaid dress. She wasn't naturally flirty and wasn't very sexually experienced. Like a fool, feeling like she was betraying Heath, she'd only had sex with two men, and those men had left her unsatisfied and wanting Heath all the more.

This weekend though, Leah was determined to go from *wanting* her gorgeous hunk of a Marine to *having* him. The first step to making that happen was her appearance, and she was certain she'd impress. Her hair and makeup were flawless, thanks to stylist Madison Roth, and her cornflower blue bridesmaid dress fit perfectly, with the bodice showcasing the girls nicely.

Mostly, Heath regarded her as family. He'd taught her how to tie her shoes, for Pete's sake. But she had caught him checking her out a couple of times, his gaze lingering on her breasts. Heath liked her breasts? If she had her way this weekend, he'd have an all access pass to breasts, and whatever else he wanted. And that meant she would have access to all of him, too.

She wanted access to everything Heath—those beautiful hazel eyes that were more green than brown, his sculpted six pack, strong, protective arms that could easily carry her curves anywhere he wanted and what she knew would be an impressive cock. Thinking of him naked and hers for the taking had her heart racing and tingling all over.

Before she lost herself in a Heath fantasy, she turned at the sound of heels clicking on the slate vestibule floor with Hannah Hailey rushing toward them.

A serious expression was on the event planner's face.

Hannah came to a stop in front of Cassie. "I hope you don't mind, but there's a little last-minute change in the procession."

Leah wasn't concerned about what the *little* change was because all she saw were Heath and Luke striding toward them. Her reaction to Heath was always the same. Her body went up in flames. Even at the office, which was more than a little embarrassing. Shit, but she had it bad for the man.

Leah couldn't help but notice Abbey's reaction to seeing Luke Stryker, the Chicago Cobras' star pitcher after ten years. Just as she expected: anger and longing. Abbey was Cassie's younger sister and Luke's ex.

There was no time to worry about those two. Leah focused on a certain delectable, former Marine and groomsman looking much too tempting in his black tails. The tuxedo jacket fit perfectly across Heath's broad shoulders and the cornflower blue bowtie, vest, and boutonniere complemented his dark blond hair and warm complexion.

Oblivious to everything and everyone else around her, she stood mesmerized as Heath approached her, wearing that sexy, smirky grin that always caused her body to react. Even with high heels she still had to crane her neck to look him in the eyes.

Her body lit up as he made slow work of sensually appraising her from head to toe. His nostrils flared, and she thought she saw lust in his greenish gaze. Her mouth went dry. Was he turned on? By *her*?

Heath gazed down at her so intensely she'd bet he could see through to her soul. "There's been a change of plans, little girl. Luke and I are walking you ladies down the aisle instead of standing up front with Jake."

Heath's deep, sexy baritone had her stomach

doing flips even though he'd called her "little girl". She would show him otherwise. Walking with him at the beginning of the ceremony was more than fine with her. The closer they were to each other the better.

Cassie turned to her and Abbey. "What do you two think? Wouldn't it be nice to walk down the aisle with these two handsome men?"

"I think that's a great idea," Leah blurted out. She looked up at Heath and flashed him an enthusiastic smile.

Feeling encouraged by Heath's reaction to her, when it was time for everyone to take their places, she took him by the hand and led him to their place in front of the closed vestibule doors. She hated letting go of his large strong hand to hook arms with him, but she had no choice. He glanced at her longingly before turning to face front.

Leah floated on air as he led her toward the altar and a waiting Jake, who was wearing a black top hat. She had to admit, he didn't look half bad and was sort of fun. She doubted Cassie would mind.

Before letting her go so they could each take their places, Heath whispered, "Until later, little girl."

Later? What did he mean? Leah could think of so many things she'd like to do later and none of them had to do with the wedding.

She leaned in close to Abbey after she took her place next to her. It looked like Luke had whispered something to Abbey, but she was having none of it. "What was that? And oh my God, does Luke look *hot* in his tux. Not as hot as Heath of course, but still."

Abbey glared back at her. She wasn't stupid. Abbey still had feelings for Luke, but probably didn't want to. "It's nothing. Luke's just being a jerk. I don't care how he looks or what he does. I'm going to enjoy this weekend, and he can go suck it for all I care."

Leah giggled and glanced at Heath, who was staring right back at her with lust in his eyes. "I'd like to suck a few things on Heath, that's for sure."

Abbey chuckled quietly. "Shhh, we're in a church"

"Makes no difference to me. I'd suck Heath in a church, near a church…" Leah now focused on *later* thanks to Heath's comment. And on sucking thanks to Abbey's. "Later" couldn't arrive soon enough.

Leah panicked when Jake took off toward Cassie and her father Phil thinking he'd changed his mind about getting married. It turned out Jake was so emotional seeing Cassie in her wedding dress he'd wanted to lead her to the altar himself.

The rest of the ceremony went off without a hitch. Leah, Abbey, and many of the guests got misty-eyed when Jake kissed his bride. She'd never seen her big brother happier. She was thrilled for them both and for the little niece or nephew who was on the way.

She'd also never been more turned on in her life. Throughout the ceremony Heath had sent lusty, heated glances in her direction. He was driving her crazy. She couldn't believe after so many years of pining over him, he was finally noticing her. And he looked damned sexy in the stupid black top hat the guys were alternating wearing.

Needing to cool down after being so close to Heath while wedding pictures were taken, she sipped on sparkling cranberry juice in Fellowship Hall. She needed a break from her hunky Marine before she embarrassed herself in front of all the ceremony guests. She was that wound up.

Leah scanned the refreshment table, wondering what to nibble on before everyone headed to dinner at Cucina Antonetti's Elmhurst location. Not wanting to spoil her appetite for what she knew would be delectable Italian food served up family style, she opted for fruit and a peanut butter cookie.

Finding Cassie happily chatting with several guests across the room, Leah sat at a table with a few guests she didn't know chatting away and munching on sweet treats. She cut into her cantaloupe and was about to take bite when Heath sat down next to her.

"What do you have there, little girl?"

Oh shit. Heath was still wearing the top hat and looking much tastier than her snacks. Her body immediately went into overdrive. Her skin warmed, and her nipples hardened.

She pulled herself together as best as she could. "Just some snacks before dinner." She hoped she sounded casual and unaffected.

Heath's smirky grin sent her pulse racing. "Can I have a bite of your cookie?"

She gasped. What was Heath doing? Was he coming on to her in the middle of Fellowship Hall?

She picked up her peanut butter cookie with a shaky hand and held it up to Heath's tempting lips. He took a large bite and slowly chewed, his greenish brown eyes never leaving hers. She watched him lick the crumbs from his luscious lips and craved a taste of those lips for herself.

"Mmmm. Sweet and delicious."

He moved in a little closer, like he wanted to kiss her. She was all in. She didn't care where they were.

"So, Heath, how are things at Cobras HQ these days?" an older gentleman with a receding hairline and navy-blue suit asked.

"Very well. I was recently promoted to finance director. And Jake's younger sister Leah here is one of my best financial analysts." Heath turned to her and winked. Winked! What was he doing?

Heath's recent promotion had been a big deal. His road to recovery after getting injured in Afghanistan hadn't been easy, but he'd done the work. When he'd felt physically able and emotionally ready, he'd taken his love of numbers and earned his finance degree. Just as she had.

The Stryker family had owned the baseball team since its inception in 1927, with Luke's Uncle Darren its current owner. The Strykers were as close as family. The Cobras' organization was a diversity and veteran friendly employer. She, Heath, her brother Jake, who was one of their corporate attorneys, and her new sister-in-law Cassie, a marketing manager had to endure the same grueling interview process every other employee did. And they were also required to sign the same stringent employment contract. There were no *free rides* for family.

"You really think I'm one of your best analysts?" It meant so much to her to hear him say that. She worked hard, even as an intern during school breaks. The Cobras' organization was an amazing place to work, with wonderful benefits and a waiting list for open positions. The organization treated their employees well, regardless of their title, but expected a lot from them in return.

"Absolutely, little girl. You always have been. Especially to me." Heath's penetrating gaze made her heart soar.

I think you're the best, too.

****

Heath sat beside Leah at the head table in Jake and Cassie's banquet room at Cucina Antonetti's. The seating arrangement was part of Luke's mission to win his ex and longtime love Abbey back. It turned out Luke's three-year love affair with Hollywood "It" girl

Brenna Sinclair had been a farce all along, and he was determined to win Abbey back for good this weekend.

He waited with all the wedding guests for dinner service to begin. He wasn't sure what the fuck he was doing. He'd been openly flirting with Leah, and she had been receptive. Not that he was surprised. He didn't think she'd refuse his advances.

The woman had crushed on him since she was a little girl and he knew it, although he'd never done anything to encourage her. She was one of his best friend's sister. You don't get involved with a friend's sister. Everyone knows that, but it didn't change how he felt.

He was conflicted. He wanted Leah so much he'd been half hard most of the day. He'd chastised himself and felt guilty for wanting her at all. *Fuck.* Why did he let Jake and Luke's Uncle Darren's comments while they got ready for the wedding get in his head?

He'd thought his feelings for Leah had been a secret, but he'd found out they hadn't been. Jake had even given his blessing if he wanted to pursue Leah, as long as he made an honest effort to make things work. Heath couldn't have been more surprised.

Just because he wanted her and he knew she had feelings for him, didn't mean they *should* be together. Even with Jake giving him the green light. What if after she got to know him more intimately she ran the other way? And what if she realized she didn't want to be with a hearing-impaired Marine with combat nightmares and other emotional issues from his time in the service? Shit, how he hated the acronym PTSD. He hated what it was even more.

He stared at his champagne glass filled with Moët & Chandon Dom Perignon White Gold, courtesy of Luke, and wondered if he shouldn't just cut his losses and go back to the status quo with her.

"Now that everyone's glasses are filled, the best man and maid of honor can come on up for the toasts, and then dinner service will start," the DJ announced.

Leah placed a hand on his forearm. Her delicate touch made his cock jerk. *Damn it.* "Do you know what Luke will say? Did he share his speech with you guys?"

Heath looked at her. She had the face of an angel, and her deep brown eyes were dilated. Christ, he wanted her so much he ached with it. *What the fuck am I going to do? What if she gets hurt? I couldn't live with myself if that happened.*

"No, he didn't say anything to us about it." He couldn't look away from the woman who'd been his obsession for so long. Luke began speaking, but Heath wasn't paying much attention until Luke mentioned something about not being able to share embarrassing stories about Jake and their top-secret mission.

"Sorry, everyone, but my top-secret mission request clearly states I can't." Luke held up the mission request he'd received from Jake.

Heath quickly retrieved his own mission request from his tuxedo pants pocket. "Mine too!" Heath held up the note and waved it for everyone to see.

From what he was able to discern, no one seemed aware Luke had hurt the shit out of his shoulder on his pitching arm in a recent motorcycle accident. He'd sworn them all to secrecy about his injury and was wearing a shoulder support under his clothes when he probably should have been wearing a sling instead.

Luke continued on with his speech, and Leah leaned into Heath, her soft, full tits pressing against his arm. He was so hard and ready for her he could have fucked her on top of the head table and not given a shit if everyone watched.

If he pursued her, she'd learn he could be an exhibitionist when it came to sex and play. And how would she react to *that*? The filthy, kinky details about him she didn't know, added to his military service issues, could scare her off and then he'd have nothing. It could even destroy their lifelong friendship, and he couldn't live with that.

She looked at him with those doe eyes of hers. Her love shone so bright his heart constricted. "I had no idea about this mission thing. Can I see it?"

Unable to deny her, he passed her the note. He watched, transfixed as she read the Project Tyler mission with a sweet smile on her face. Shit, he loved her so much. What the hell was he going to do?

She looked back at him, her smile beaming. "This is so clever. It's a combination of *Mission Impossible* and *Taken*. Jake never said anything about this. Did you guys have a beer before the ceremony?"

All he could do was nod, he was that dumbstruck by his Leah. *His*. Leah wanted to be his, and all he had to do was claim her.

"Not during though. I don't recall seeing any beer bottles in church."

Suddenly the room erupted in applause. He was startled out of their little bubble. The speeches were apparently over. He and Leah both applauded as Abbey and Luke returned to the head table. They'd missed most of the speeches after Luke mentioned him as his older brother, too caught up in each other. He was all right with that. He'd catch everything on the wedding DVD.

Turning back to Leah he took the note back from her. "No, not during the ceremony. I doubt Cassie would have minded." Cassie was easygoing and even-tempered. She was perfect for Jake.

And although Leah may not know it, *she* was

perfect for *him*. She always had been. Even as a young girl. She had been only eight years old when he'd joined the Marines at eighteen. The letters and care packages she'd sent during his ten years in the service meant more to him than anything else.

He'd kept every letter and every item that wasn't perishable. Even her brown teddy bear, Bentley. He'd given it to her when she was three years old, and she'd taken it with her everywhere she went. It must have been difficult for her to part with it, but for him, she had. He treasured her and everything she'd done for him.

Heath also knew how hurt she was after he'd been injured and had chosen to recover in Texas at his unit's Sergeant Major Trace Baker's Angus cattle ranch. His unit's Gunnery Sergeant Bill Foster lived close by in a home on an organic livestock ranch.

He hadn't mentioned Rapture and Envy, Texas, by name to his family or friends. South of Dallas, Rapture was a unique small town that welcomed all people, persuasions, and comprised many alternative families. Trace and his brother Logan had three fathers. Heath hadn't judged. He cared about the Baker family. They had been welcoming and understanding after he'd been discharged and was broken, inside and out. He'd had his first exposure to BDSM at Club Envidious in Rapture's sister city, Envy.

Heath smiled at the beautiful woman in front of him who'd captured his heart so long ago. "Cassie's the one for Jake, no doubt about it." *And maybe you're the one for me.*

He fucking hated being so indecisive. Damn Jake and Darren. They should have just kept their opinions and suggestions to themselves.

Dinner service began giving him a slight reprieve from over-thinking this thing with Leah. He was starved and intended on treating himself to some delicious Italian food and "white" carbs which he usually limited. He planned on indulging in desserts for a change, too. *Nothing would taste as sweet as Leah though.*

Damn it.

Heath enjoyed watching Leah appreciate her food. He couldn't stand stick thin women who only ate lettuce. She wasn't overweight by any means, but she had delectable curves he craved to get his hands on.

"All right, folks, as you can see the sweet table is just about ready for everyone. Enjoy," the DJ announced.

Leah's shy smile had him hardening in his pants again. "I could definitely go for some dessert. What about you?"

He was on board with having *her* for dessert. Little temptress. He noticed Luke and Jake stand. Luke leaned over and called to him. "We're getting desserts to share with the ladies. You want to come along and get some for you and Leah?"

Leah beamed and nodded. "That's a great idea. Do you mind, Heath?"

Hell, he'd would bring the entire sweet table over if that's what she wanted. He had it that bad, though he still wasn't sure he should. *Man up, Marine, for fuck's sake!*

Leah gazed at him expectantly, waiting for him to answer. He offered a small smile and nodded. "Yeah, sounds like a good idea."

As he, Jake, and Luke approached the dessert table, Rocco rose from his seat next to Hannah and joined them in line. He'd noticed the heated glances they'd shared throughout dinner. Heath liked Hannah and thought she'd be a good match for the Italian. Why Rocco insisted on denying his attraction to the event planner, he didn't know. *Probably because he suffers from a lot of the same issues you do.*

Luke's phone chimed in his pants with a text message. Not even trying to be subtle, he, Jake, and Rocco looked over Luke's shoulder at his phone. The text was from Brenna Sinclair. They exchanged a few quick messages, and Luke put his phone away.

Jake shook his head and spoke to the group. "Don't bother asking him, guys, he's not going to tell us anything."

Ignoring Jake, Luke turned to Rocco. "So, how are things going with Hannah?"

Rocco looked down at his shoes and shrugged. Heath had never seen the man blush before, but there he was. Blushing over Hannah.

Rocco looked up and glared at Jake. "Interesting seating arrangement."

Jake held his hands up in surrender. "Don't look at *me*. Cassie did the seating arrangements before you and Hannah met. It worked out though. Admit it."

Rocco just shrugged, looking unsure. Heath could relate.

"Look, just get some desserts and share with her. You too, Heath," Luke suggested.

"Luke's right," Jake said.

Heath was still fucking undecided, and he needed to decide soon. He was acting ridiculous.

Rocco didn't seem sure either. Luke sighed. "Look, how about you guys consider this a part of your *own* reboot weekend like Abbey said in her speech? She's agreed to let me reboot with her this weekend."

Heath was stunned. "But you're looking for more than a weekend though," he said.

"I know that, but Abbey's been running hot and cold on me all day. I got her to agree to the weekend at least. She doesn't understand that I intend on getting *all* of them. Yet," Luke replied.

Heath considered that while they moved up in the dessert buffet line. Maybe the weekend was all he and Leah needed to get each other out of their systems. He doubted it. He knew once he had a taste of her he wouldn't want to ever let her go. And *that* was the problem.

• Chapter Three

Leah couldn't quite believe how the day was playing out with Heath. He had to know he was driving her crazy with need. She wasn't sure what was going on in his head, but she loved this flirty, sexual side of him.

"Here, have another bite of strawberry cheesecake." He held the fork to her lips.

She couldn't care less if anyone saw them. She wanted the women who'd been eyeing him all day to see he was focused on her and her alone. *In your face, bitches!*

She opened her mouth and accepted the sweet, creamy treat he offered her. She moaned, it was so delicious, and watched happily as he stared intently at her mouth as she chewed. Slowly, she licked her lips, and his gaze followed the trail her tongue took. She'd never felt more sexy or desired in her life.

The smoldering look in his eyes sent her pulse racing. Screw it, she would kiss him. She'd take her chance and see what happened. The mischievous grin on his rugged face was all the invitation she needed. *Good. He wants to kiss me, too.* She didn't know why, but she also didn't want to question his motives. Maybe he'd come to his senses and saw her as a potential partner and not a little sister.

Leah leaned in to test the waters, and he leaned in toward her. *Yes!*

They both startled and pulled away when the DJ's booming voice played over the room's speaker system. "All right, everyone, we're going to get the evening's festivities underway. The photographers have set up in the corner next to the gift table for anyone who would like to have pictures taken. Jake and Cassie, come on up for your first dance as man and wife."

"That was shitty timing," Heath mumbled.

Leah couldn't help but smile. Now she was sure he wanted to kiss her. Heath scooted his chair closer to hers and took her small hand and placed it into his larger, more powerful one. The tiny scars on his hands were a visible testament to his bravery and sacrifice during his time in the Marines. Leah knew he had others that most people would never see, on his arms, chest, and back. To her, his external scars made him even more beautiful.

Heath's warmth filled her with a longing she'd never known. Only he had ever had this effect on her. Leah's heart was so full it overwhelmed her.

They sat together hand in hand and watched the newlyweds dance their first dance as man and wife. Cassie and Jake had selected "The Way You Look Tonight" by Tony Bennett as their first song. Tears sprang to Leah's eyes watching them. Her brother and his new wife exuded love and happiness. Leah couldn't count how many times she had fantasized about being in Jake and Cassie's place with Heath.

"Hey, what's wrong, little girl?" Heath brushed her tears away with his warm fingers. His touch was addictive. She craved it everywhere.

Leah leaned into him and smiled. "They're beautiful, don't you think?"

Heath's intense gaze made her heart flutter wildly. "You're beautiful, little girl," he whispered so softly she strained to hear him over the music.

"Me?" He thought she was beautiful? She had no idea he felt that way. She thought he was beautiful, too.

"Fuck, yeah."

She didn't hesitate and kissed him lightly. His lips felt warm and perfect against hers. The delicate contact had her head swimming. She wanted so much more. Needed so much more.

"If the bridal party and parents of the bride and groom would like to come to the dance floor now, please," the DJ requested.

Reluctantly they pulled apart from each other. "I'm going to kill this fucking DJ," Heath muttered under his breath.

She couldn't help but giggle. She had to admit it did something for her ego knowing he was irritated at being interrupted.

He frowned at her. "It's not funny, little girl."

She stood when she saw Luke and Abbey head onto the dance floor. She extended a hand to him. "Come dance with me, Marine."

She was ecstatic. She'd never danced with Heath before. She wanted to feel his strong body against hers, even if they wore clothes—for now. If his interaction with her so far today was any indication, who knew where the night would lead? She knew where *she* wanted it to lead. Naked and in a bed. Hers or his, she didn't care which.

Heath blew out a frustrated breath and stood. After he took her hand, she led him to the dance floor where everyone was dancing to the end of "The Way You Look Tonight".

With his strong arm around her waist and his hand firmly in hers, they slowly swayed to "Unforgettable" by Nat King Cole. Though Leah's other hand lay on his shoulder, she wanted to run her hands through his thick blond locks.

Lust shone through his greenish brown gaze, and Leah felt compelled to ask what she'd wondered all day. "What's going on with you today? Not that I mind, but…"

He pulled her in close, and she felt his erection

press against her belly. He was long and thick like she knew he would be. She wanted him so badly she ached. Her breasts felt heavy and her nipples were so hard she was grateful to be pressed up against Heath so no one could see them poking against the bodice of her dress.

He closed his eyes briefly. "You drive me fucking crazy I want you so much."

Leah's heart raced and rejoiced. "You do?"

He ground his erection into her a little harder. She needed to get him alone as quickly as possible before he changed his mind.

"I have for a long time, little girl."

He did? That was news to her. He had always treated her platonically. And that had bothered the crap out of her. "Unforgettable" was ending, and she needed alone time with him. She took him by the hand, ready to find someplace private.

"All right, everyone. The dance floor is now open to all. Don't be shy. Let's get this party started," the DJ bellowed out.

Suddenly they were surrounded by enthusiastic wedding guests as a fast tempo dance number began. Feeling like they had no choice, they joined the happy wedding guests and danced along.

"We'll talk in a little while." He nearly shouted to her so she could hear him over the dance music.

She smiled and nodded. She wanted to do so much more than talk, but talking was a start. She couldn't help but be amused when her little cousin Amy, the flower girl, asked Luke to dance and Abbey took that as her opportunity to get away from him.

Although Leah wanted to get Heath alone, she was having a wonderful time celebrating Jake and Cassie's special day. Her Marine could move on the dance floor, but she was eager to see his moves *off* the dance floor as well.

Leah saw Abbey speaking to Mel Johnson, a corporate attorney for the Cobras, near the bar. Mel was nice enough and attractive. He'd asked Leah to dinner twice, but she'd declined. It was nothing against him personally. He just wasn't Heath.

Luke noticed Abbey speaking with Mel and, as gracefully as he could, guided Amy over to her and Heath to continue dancing with. They each took one of Amy's hands and danced with the giggling, bouncing five year old between them. She imagined for a moment that Amy was theirs. *This is what it would be like for us to dance with our own daughter.*

The thought warmed her heart. She believed he would make a wonderful father.

Amy's parents retrieved their little girl, and Leah found herself again in Heath's arms swaying to "It's Your Love" by Tim McGraw. Did he even realize he was holding *her* heart so tight? She held on to him, never wanting to let go.

His body felt strong, hard and warm against hers. She felt pride in the fact his cock was hard again and pressing insistently against her. Never did she imagine she could elicit such a reaction from him. Until today, he hadn't ever let on he had romantic feelings toward her at all. She wasn't sure what to make of it all.

When the song ended, he whispered in her ear, "Let's get out of here so we can talk."

She was on board for private time. She wanted to do so much more than talk. Happily, she let him lead her out of the banquet room into the hall.

Luke's security detail was standing to their right with Rocco further down the hall, all of them staring at a closed door. Several others were milling around in the hallway trying to look inconspicuous with their eyes trained on the closed door. Leah wasn't sure what was going on. Was it the press? Were they all in the room at the end of the hall?

Still holding her hand, Heath led Leah toward the closest security guard. "What the hell is going on? Is Luke all right? Is the press here?"

Always the protector. That was Heath.

Luke's security guard shook his head. "No. Mr. Stryker is fine. He's in the small room at the end of the hall with Ms. Jayne. They were arguing—loudly. At the moment they're not shouting."

"What about everyone else in the hallway acting as if they're not interested in what's going on?" Heath asked. He scowled at some of the restaurant patrons milling around and a few were intimidated and returned to Cucina Antonetti's main restaurant dining room.

The security guard wore a smirk as he watched several restaurant guests leave the hallway toward the restaurant. "They haven't been unruly or intrusive. For now, we're leaving them alone. The restrooms are in this hallway as you know."

That was true, she considered. They couldn't make the restrooms off limits because Luke and Abbey were holed up in a banquet room together.

Heath sighed. "Are there any other empty banquet rooms available?"

Leah's heart picked up speed, and her stomach did little flips. She would finally be alone with Heath. She preferred they were alone somewhere with a bed, but at this point she'd take whatever she could get.

The security guard pointed to a room behind them down a short hallway that led outside. "Yes, sir. That one is free."

He strode toward the empty banquet room with purpose and her in tow. "If anything changes out here, come get me," he called out behind them.

After they entered the small banquet room that held five tables done up with white table cloths and white napkins at each chair, Heath slammed the banquet doors closed and had her backed up against the nearest cherry wood paneled wall before she knew what was happening. He crushed his lips against hers, his tongue demanding entry. She was surprised she was so turned on by his alpha display.

She happily acquiesced, and Heath took possession of her mouth. His tongue relentlessly tangled with hers until she became so drunk with lust her knees nearly gave out. She held him around the neck and felt him slide his hands down from her waist and grip her ass cheeks and squeeze. He ground his rock-hard dick against her stomach, and her pussy contracted. One of them groaned, she wasn't sure who, before they ended their kiss, both panting.

He touched his forehead to hers and held her tight. "You drive me fucking crazy, Leah."

She couldn't help but smile. He drove her crazy, too, in every dirty, sexy, lustful way possible. "What's going on with you? Us?"

He sighed and let her go. He stepped back slightly and took her hands away from around his neck, holding them gently in his. She immediately regretted asking him anything. She wanted him close. Needed him close. She ached for him, had for years.

He shook his head seemingly conflicted. "I'm not entirely sure, but I know I want you, Leah. So much I ache with it. But I know I shouldn't and I'm not sure what the fuck to do about it and it's pissing me off."

Her heart soared. The man she'd loved her entire life was admitting to wanting her. Though not a declaration of love, she knew he cared about her. She also knew better than to gush about her undying love right now.

She looked up into his sorrowful but caring gaze. She didn't want him to have any doubts regarding the two of them together. She knew deep in her heart they belonged together. She was certain that with a little time he would come to know and believe it, too. Although she didn't want to, she needed to take things slow. Ease him into the idea of the two of them together.

She smiled at him, hoping she appeared calm and collected. "I think you must know I want you, too. Why shouldn't you want me? I don't understand." She had a good idea why. Because Heath and Jake were close friends. Brothers. And you don't mess with your friend's little sister, right?

Fuck that. She and Heath were adults. If they wanted to be together her brother better not get in the way. Her brother Jake had more than enough to keep him busy—a new bride, a baby on the way, and a job with the Cobras that kept him on his toes. Where she and Heath were concerned, Jake needed to mind his own business and stay out of it.

"I think you know why, little girl. At least partially." Heath kissed her gently. She was so into him any affection sent her body into overdrive. She was burning up, needing him to get over his aversion toward at least fucking her as soon as possible. She could only take so much.

"Does it have to matter I'm Jake's sister? I'm a grown woman now. I'm sure you've noticed. Jake doesn't get to decide who I'm with. I do."

She wondered if knowing him all of her life was a disadvantage rather than an advantage as she'd always thought. Would he have doubts about her if they had just met?

"I don't want to do anything to jeopardize a long and important friendship. We're all like family, don't you agree?" Heath looked down at her expectantly.

She agreed with his assessment about their close-knit ties. But she didn't agree it should stop them from becoming even closer. She knew her family loved Heath like their own. She didn't believe for a minute they'd be upset if they got together. Even Jake, eventually. Once he got over the "bro code" crap.

A thought occurred to her that had her stomach knotting. Heath had known her since the day she was *born*.

"You never changed my diapers or gave me a bath when I was a baby, did you?" She would be mortified if he had. He had a younger sister, Sylvia, who was thirty-one years old. He'd probably helped his mother with *her* care. If he had helped her family with her care as a baby, he might consider any sexual or romantic relationship incestuous in some way. *Shit.* That might be why he still referred to her as "little girl".

Tears pricked at her eyes as she considered how he might feel. She let go of his hands and tried to get around him to leave the banquet room.

Heath didn't let her get very far. He deftly picked her up by the waist, kicked a chair the away from the table nearest to them, and promptly placed her down on top of it with her legs dangling over the edge. He placed a finger under her chin and tilted it up so she was looking directly into his gorgeous greenish eyes.

"Grown women don't cut and run, do they? You said you're a grown woman. Grown women stay and talk things through, right?"

Leah nodded. She didn't trust herself not to say something foolish. *Act like an adult, Leah.*

"To answer your questions, no, I never changed

your diapers or gave you a bath. Your family was very protective of you, even with me. Not that I blame them. Our family was the same with Sylvia."

She managed a small smile. She liked Heath's sister, Sylvia, and her husband, Greg. They ran a successful dental practice in Elmhurst with Heath's father, Douglas.

"All right, that's a relief. Jake's a big boy though. He'll have to get over it if we decide to get together. You don't really think Jake would end a lifelong friendship, do you?" She didn't want to cause Heath's friendship with Jake to end because of her. In her mind, it shouldn't have to.

He took her small hands in his powerful ones and squeezed gently. Her body warmed. God, she loved him so much.

He shook his head. "No. Apparently my feelings toward you haven't been much of a secret. Jake gave me his blessing if I wanted to pursue you."

Really? He did? When? Hope bloomed in her heart. "Then I don't understand why you're still unsure." She brought their joined hands to her chest near her heart. She hoped he could feel it racing. A heart that had loved him her entire life.

"There's our ten-year age difference for one. You're young with your whole life ahead of you, and I feel old and broken compared to you. I'm not whole anymore. You deserve someone perfect, like you. And we work together, so we'd have to report our relationship to HR. What would happen if things didn't work out between us? Would you feel forced to leave? Would I? If we chose to stay, would working together be uncomfortable and awkward?"

She had considered everything he had. All except the part about him being broken and imperfect. To her,

Heath was perfect. She didn't think less of him because of his hearing loss. She knew sign language.

"A ten-year age difference at this point doesn't mean much. I'd like to think we're mature enough that if something happened we could still work together. We've both worked hard for our positions at the Cobras."

Leah let go of Heath's hands and stood up. She looked up at the man who meant more to her than anyone in the world. "You're not broken. To me, you're perfect just the way you are. I'm far from perfect, and you know it. And shouldn't *I* be the one who decides what and who I deserve?"

Heath put his arms around her and held her tight. Leah felt his semi-hard cock pressed against her. She was elated. Even though he had doubts, he still wanted her. They'd just have to take things slow. Until he felt confident they could have a future together.

"What if my hearing deteriorates and hearing aids or cochlear implants can't help me? How will you feel then?"

Leah's heart ached for him. Did he truly believe his hearing was what made him worth loving?

"I learned sign while you were in Texas recovering. I can handle it." Leah hoped like hell she was getting through to him.

He lightly stroked her back, sending shivers up and down her spine. "That's my point. You shouldn't have to deal with my condition at all. You shouldn't have had to learn how to sign. You can have someone better, uninjured. You deserve that."

"I deserve *you*. Are you saying that the men and women who get injured during deployments should lose their partners? They should cut and run, as you put it?" She didn't want to believe he felt that way. The men and women who served were heroes. They shouldn't be cast aside if they got injured.

Heath extricated himself from their hug. She mourned the loss of his strength and warmth. He put his hands in his pockets and looked at Leah with such sorrow and pain she wanted to cry. Her warrior was a tortured soul, and she wanted nothing more than to ease his burdens.

"No. Of course not. You're right. Sometimes I wish things were different. That *I* was different. Even without the hearing loss and other scars, war changes you. The memories, the trauma, even nightmares stay with you long after you've left the battlefield. I've seen things that can never be unseen. Done things that can never be undone."

She rubbed his arms, offering what little comfort she could. Even through the tuxedo jacket sleeves his arms exuded strength and power. He was not a damaged man. Not to her. Heath just needed to believe it, too.

"I know that. I wouldn't think otherwise. I wish things were different, too. But let's make the most of what we have right now. Let's go back to the Fairchild Hotel, and we can make new memories. Better memories. Together." *Come on, Heath, give us a shot.*

Heath chuckled and graced her with a mischievous grin. He held her tightly and ground his now rock-hard cock against her. Maybe they could use this banquet room and then head to the hotel? She didn't know if she could wait much longer to finally have him inside her.

"Ready to fuck me, are you?"

"You know I am. I've wanted you for a long time, and you know that." Heath's dirty talk was such an unexpected turn-on. She'd bet he was aggressive in bed, and she couldn't wait to find out.

He had been kind but dismissive toward her

clumsy overtures over the years. It hadn't diminished her feelings toward him though. She might be naïve, but she'd always believed he'd eventually come around.

He broke their embrace and looked at her with a regretful expression on his handsome face. Her heart sank. Had he changed his mind?

"I'd like nothing better than to get you in bed and inside that sweet pussy of yours. But it's still early. We can't just leave. We're a part of a small bridal party. We need to stay a while longer. I think we'd both regret leaving too early—as much as we want to right now."

She sighed and shrugged. She knew he was right. She'd been looking forward to Jake's wedding day and so far, including this private time with Heath, she'd been having a wonderful time.

"I know. What do you think we should do then?"

Heath took her by the hand, leading her to the closed banquet room doors. "I think we should stay a while longer, enjoy the evening with everyone else. Then let's give ourselves the rest of the weekend to see if we want to pursue something more than some hot, hard fucking. Maybe the weekend is all we'll need to get each other out of our systems and we continue on like before."

She didn't think she'd want to go back to being just platonic friends after the weekend was over, but she didn't want to push her luck. He could be right. Maybe once they got together they'd decide they were better off as friends. Her heart told her it probably wouldn't be the case though.

"All right. Let's give the weekend a try and see what happens," she conceded. It was a start, more than she'd ever had with him up to this point.

"There's a lot you don't know about me, little girl. Sexually, I mean. If we decide to go past the weekend, I hope you don't get scared off."

Oh yeah? That got her attention. Thoughts of Club Envidious's owner Kyle Asher, the Dom, came to Leah's mind. Cassie had met him at the Golden Horns during their soft opening. He owned it and was bringing his "entertainment company" to the area. She could so picture her warrior as a Dom. She didn't know if that's what Heath meant, but she was willing to find out.

"I guess we'll wait and see what we decide at the end of the weekend," she replied.

"In the meantime, to hold me over until I get you back to the hotel, give me your panties."

What? "You want them *now*? As in I spend the rest of the reception without them on?" She had done nothing like that before. It was sexy and exciting. It would be their little secret.

"Exactly."

He held out his hand and waited. Giddy with excitement and a little nervous, she pulled her bridesmaid dress up so she could reach underneath and take her panties off. She knew they were damp with her arousal. She was shaking and caught them on one of her heels trying to get them off. Heath held on to her waist, steadying her so she could snag them free.

She handed Heath her panties and righted herself. She'd purchased the expensive white lace and satin bra and panty set hoping to show them off to him. Her heart was racing as she watched him bring them to his nose and inhale deeply. *Oh my God! So hot.*

He pocketed her panties and opened the banquet room doors. "Thank you, little girl. I know that was scary for you." He took her hand and led her through the banquet room doors. "Let's get back to the party and have some fun."

• Chapter Four

Heath stood outside the wedding banquet room doors shooting the shit with Jake and his brother-in-law Greg about a quarter to midnight. Although he could have been balls deep inside Leah long before now, he was glad they'd stayed at the reception.

It meant a lot to him to see his little "brother" Jake so fucking happy he was wearing a goofy grin on his face along with that stupid top hat as his wedding day ended. He was proud of Jake. He was a good man, had married a wonderful woman, and would make an amazing father. Heath tried to ignore the pang of jealousy in his gut.

I want what Jake has. I could have it with Leah. I know she loves me.

He pushed aside for now the thoughts of him and Leah together with a family. He didn't want to get ahead of himself. He wasn't sure if a weekend with her was a good idea or not or if anything more would come of it. He needed to take things one fucking step at a time. For his sake and hers.

"I should warn you, Sylvia noticed you and Leah tonight. I think she's been looking at wedding venues on her phone," Greg said, smirking.

Jake, his asshole little brother, chuckled. "It's about time you got your head out of your ass, big brother."

Heath scowled at them both and shook his head. He'd spent the evening feeling Leah's panties in his pants pocket. He'd been in a semi-hard state all night knowing she was bare under her pretty bridesmaid dress. He knew she'd been nervous about giving them to him. She was a good girl at heart but willing to be bad for *him*.

He craved her goodness, badness, and everything in between. And it scared the shit of out him because he knew once he got a taste of her, he'd never want to let her go. If they went past this weekend and she changed her mind about him later down the line, it would wreck him. Although he knew the risks, he couldn't walk away.

"Yeah well, you better rein her in, Greg. Tell Sylvia not to pick out china patterns or plan a bridal shower and shit. I'm still not sure if starting something with Leah is a good idea or not."

Greg just laughed. "Have you met your sister? She adores Leah and would love nothing better than for you to settle down. You know how protective she's been since you were discharged."

Heath knew all too well. Sylvia and his mother had been frantic after he'd been injured. Not that he blamed them. The Battle for Sangin was an extended campaign during the war in Afghanistan. Sangin was considered the bloodiest battleground by the British and U.S. alike, with the IED threat greater there than anywhere else in Afghanistan. He'd been "lucky", only losing his hearing and sustaining other minor injuries from which he bore the scars. Both nations had suffered the loss of over one hundred, his and Rocco's units included, and hundreds more suffered moderate to severe injuries.

It hadn't helped the family's frame of mind when he'd chosen to recover and recuperate in Texas rather than at home. Once he'd returned home, Sylvia and his mother were protective hens. After his mother passed away three years ago from a brain aneurism in her sleep, Sylvia had stepped up her game. Heath knew she meant well, but sometimes it was too much.

Jake placed the top hat on Heath's head and smiled at him like an idiot. "Just relax, will you? Damn.

Take things slow and see how it goes. No one's going to plan your wedding just yet." Then the dickhead laughed at him. Heath flipped Jake off and Greg joined in.

The three of them turned when Leah and Sylvia emerged from the ladies' restroom arm in arm giggling like schoolgirls. *Oh shit. What did you do, Sylvia?*

Sylvia hugged Jake tight. "Congratulations, Jake. I've already said goodbye to Cassie, so I think we'll be heading out, right, hun?" She went to Greg and looked at Heath with a conspiratorial expression on her face.

Greg shook Jake's hand. "All the best to you and Cassie, Jake."

Grinning, Jake nodded. "Thanks for being here. Now if I can find my lovely bride, we should head out, too. The honeymoon suite at the Fairchild Hotel awaits." Jake waggled his eyebrows and winked.

Leah put her arm around Heath's waist and snuggled in close. He stiffened at first, not used to PDA's with her but she felt so damned good against him he relaxed and went with it. He put an arm around her shoulder and pulled her close.

"Spare us the details, Jake," Leah teased.

"Right back at ya," Jake kidded back.

Greg shook his head, grinning, took Sylvia's hand, and led her toward the exit door.

"Leah, I'll call you. That top hat is a great look on you, Heath," she called out as they left.

Heath walked Leah out to the waiting limousine courtesy of Luke after they'd said their goodbyes to Jake. He needed to get her alone. It had been a long day, but he was far from tired.

The chauffer helped Leah inside the limo, and he followed closely behind sinking into the luxurious leather seats. He had to hand it to Luke and Darren. They'd gone all out to ensure the day had been special not only for

Jake and Cassie but also for the rest of the family.

"Mr. Jackson, I'll let you know when we're a few minutes from the Fairchild," the chauffer said before closing the passenger door.

The lighting inside the limo wasn't very bright, but he could make out his beautiful weekend companion easily. Halfway through the evening he'd asked her to let her hair down. The elegant up 'do she'd worn for the ceremony and pictures looked lovely on her, but he much preferred her dark wavy tresses free and falling around her shoulders.

Heath slid next to her as she admired the small bridal toss bouquet she'd caught. He took it and placed it beside her larger bridesmaid bouquet and small evening bag on the carpeted limousine floor. He couldn't wait. He needed a taste of her. Now.

She squeaked when he lifted her off the seat and settled her on his lap. She wrapped her arms around his neck, and he claimed her lips like a starving man. Which he was. He should have fucked her in the small banquet room after they'd finished talking. She eagerly opened her mouth, their tongues colliding in a ferocious dance.

He was so hard it hurt. He was certain she could feel his throbbing dick against her leg. He couldn't wait much longer to sink inside her warm, waiting pussy.

Much to his disappointment, she broke their kiss, leaving them both panting. *Shit.* No one else had ever made him as hot or as hard as Leah did. He was so screwed.

Moving quickly before he could stop her, Leah hopped off his lap and positioned herself on the floor between his legs. The sexy gleam in her eyes had his painfully hard cock pulsing in anticipation.

She ran her hands unhurriedly up and down his thighs, the heat of her hands burning a trail. Heath stopped her when she reached for his zipper. "What do you think you're doing, little girl?" He had a good idea, but wondered if she could verbalize it.

His heart raced in his chest when she smiled seductively at him. "What do you think? I'm going to take care of this big, hard dick for you."

Damn. It was official. He was screwed. His little Leah was into dirty talk? His mind raced with all the other dirty, filthy things he'd introduce her to if they went past the weekend. *Don't get ahead of yourself, pal. One step at a time.*

Acting more relaxed than he felt, he played along. He made himself comfortable in the limo seat and spread his legs a little further apart for her. He unbuttoned his pants and slowly unzipped them. She watched him with such a lust he considered laying her flat on the limousine floor and fucking her hard before they reached the Fairchild Hotel.

"So, you think you can wrap those luscious lips around my big fat cock, little girl?" Heath wasn't small. He wanted to see how much of him she could handle.

Even in the dim interior of the car, he could see her dilated pupils. His Leah wanted to suck his dick. He would let her for a little bit. The first time he came inside her would be in her tight, little pussy, not her mouth.

She wasted no time and pulled on his boxer briefs, freeing his cock. The warmth of her delicate hand wrapped around his length nearly set him off. Where was his legendary control?

"Let's find out," she purred.

She licked the pre-cum from the tip of his dick, and he almost lost it. How did she do this to him? "Go on, suck me."

He held on to Leah's head, his fingers tangled in her thick, silky locks. She swallowed his cock as far as she could. The feel of her hot mouth engulfing his length was so fucking incredible he groaned and pushed himself deeper. To his surprise, she deep-throated him completely and hummed. The vibration practically had him coming right then and there.

Leah sucked him with enthusiasm, finding the perfect rhythm. He gripped her hair tighter, eliciting a groan from her. She liked a little pain? He could definitely work with that.

The base of his spine tingled. He needed to stop her, but her mouth felt too fucking good.

"Mr. Jackson, we're near the Fairchild," the chauffeur's voice announced through the limo's speakers.

Leah pulled off his throbbing dick with a pop, and he immediately missed her warm mouth. Shit, he was done for. He needed to get inside of her. Now.

"I'm sorry I didn't get to finish. I wanted to take care of you." She frowned, collected her bouquets, evening bag and sat down beside him, snuggling close.

"It's all right. I wanted to come buried deep inside you anyway," Heath said as he tucked himself back inside his pants and zipped up. He grabbed the top hat that had fallen off while Leah was blowing him and put it back on.

The moment the limousine came to a complete stop at the Fairchild Hotel, he was out the door extending a hand to her. She emerged with her bouquets and evening bag in tow. Taking her bag in one hand, and then grasping her now free hand in the other, he escorted her past the smiling chauffer and into the hotel lobby.

"Have a good evening, Mr. Jackson," the chauffer called out.

"I intend to."

Leah giggled as her high heels clicked against the

marble floors. Wasting no time, he hurried to the golden elevator banks with her following alongside him. His stomach clenched when he saw three of Luke's security detail positioned near the elevators. He had noticed nothing unusual. The hotel was quiet with two agents at the front desk casually chatting when they arrived.

"Is something wrong? I noticed nothing to be concerned about on our way here," Heath said to the security detail. He felt Leah grasp his hand. If she was afraid, she needn't be. *I'll take care of you. I won't let anything happen to you, little girl. It's why I always carry a small folding tactical knife.*

"No sir, Mr. Jackson. Mr. Stryker and Miss Jayne are due shortly. We're getting into position for their arrival," one of the security detail replied.

A set of elevator doors opened, and he motioned for Leah to step inside. "If you need me, I'll be in Miss Tyler's room." Her instant blush was adorable. She was sexy but sweet and innocent all at the same time. He had no business getting involved with her, but he couldn't stop himself.

The security detail nodded. "Yes, sir. We have the room assignments."

Heath stepped inside the elevator, tossed her evening bag on the floor and was all over Leah before the doors fully closed. Her full lush tits pressed against his chest drove him insane. He needed to get her out of her dress ASAP. He was through waiting.

She dropped her bouquets and they landed on the elevator floor with a soft thud. She wrapped her arms around him and kissed him as desperately as he kissed her. Their tongues danced and tangled until they drew apart, gasping for air.

He held her close, grinding his painfully hard dick against her stomach and slowly glided his hands from her waist to the globes of her panty-less ass. He squeezed the luscious mounds and groaned.

"I can't believe I wasn't wearing panties at my brother's wedding reception," she breathed.

He squeezed her incredible ass cheeks again and kissed her neck, inhaling the sweet vanilla scent that he'd come to know as hers. Sweet and delicious and *his*. At least for the weekend. *You want more than the weekend, and you know it.*

He chuckled against her neck and ran his tongue along her fluttering pulse. Her moan was almost his undoing. "That was our dirty little secret." He sucked on her pulsing flesh and ground his rock-hard cock against her. He nearly came in his pants. "Do you like keeping dirty secrets with me, little girl?"

"Yes," Leah whispered.

The elevator stopped at the top floor where Luke had reserved a block of rooms for friends and family. Wasting no time, he took her by the hand and led her past the waiting security detail dotted along the hallway to her room. The security detail weren't the only ones who had the room assignment list.

Heath had Leah pressed up against the wall inside her suite after tossing her things aside.

"I've been waiting all fucking day to get my hands on you, little girl." He yanked off his tuxedo jacket, tossing it aside, and pulled her bridesmaid dress skirt and slip up so he could get a good look at the sweet pussy he was going to devour.

Heath knelt down in front of the woman who'd been tormenting him the entire day and inhaled her sweet, musky essence. His mouth watered at the sight of Leah's slick cunt. He was relieved she wasn't waxed bare but neatly trimmed. All woman.

"Spread your legs for me. Hold on to your dress,"

he said looking up at her.

Her eyes grew wide, but she spread her legs for him anyway. "What? Why? What are you going to do?"

Had no other man ever tasted her pussy before? *What the fuck?* His throbbing cock ached at the thought of being the first to sample her. He needed to stop thinking of Leah as his. It was dangerous for his heart.

"What do you think, little girl? I'm going to taste this sweet pussy of yours. Hasn't anyone ever gotten a taste of you before?" he asked, knowing the obvious answer.

She shook her head and half-heartedly tried to push him away. "You don't have to. It's okay. I thought we were going to—you know."

Her shyness was adorable. He'd never wanted anyone more. "Fuck? Don't worry, we're going to. But first, I *want* to taste you. If you don't like it, I'll stop. I promise, all right?" Heath couldn't have her afraid, that wouldn't do. He needed all of her. Anything less was not acceptable.

Although her lovely face showed concern and doubt, she nodded. He didn't hesitate and got his first taste, licking her from her drenched pussy hole to her swollen clit. Her addictive tasting juices made him growl with satisfaction. He watched from his knees as she closed her eyes and leaned her head against the wall, moaning in ecstasy.

So responsive—for me.

Encouraged, Heath placed one of her legs over his shoulder and grabbed her ass, pulling her closer. With better access to her wet cunt he devoured her like the starving man he was.

Back and forth he alternated between licking Leah's entire slick slit and flicking her swollen little clit. It didn't take long before she was moaning so loudly he hoped she was heard in the hallway. She tugged on his hair, drawing him even closer to her greedy little pussy as he lapped up all her juices. He'd never get enough of her. He was done for. He was so fucking hard he thought he might come in his pants before he could get inside of her.

He felt her stiffen and then shout his name as she catapulted over the edge. Feeling pride like he'd never known before with a woman, he tenderly placed her leg back down. She stood against the wall with her eyes closed, holding her dress up to her waist with a satisfied grin on her face, panting. He felt ten feet tall.

Heath couldn't wait any longer. He needed to get inside her right fucking now. He toed off his shoes and ditched his pants and boxer briefs. He picked her up, and her eyes flew open in surprise. "Wrap your legs around me, Leah. I need you."

She quickly complied, and Heath rammed his throbbing cock inside her hot, wet pussy, pressing her firmly against the wall. They both moaned once he was balls deep inside her tight cunt. Her pussy walls gripped him like a vise.

"You're so big," she breathed.

He smiled. What man didn't like hearing *that*? He slowly pulled out and pushed back in. "And you're so fucking tight." He groaned. He didn't move, giving her a minute to adjust to his *big* dick.

"I can't believe you're fucking me. I've wanted you for so long." Leah kissed him tentatively, tasting herself on his lips.

He shoved his tongue in her mouth, giving her a real taste of her essence. She was the best thing he'd ever tasted, hands down. "You taste amazing, don't you think?" She nodded, smiling shyly. Heath pulled out and back into her tight heat, the journey a little easier now but still incredibly tight. He didn't think he'd last long. "I think so, too. Now, let's get serious about fucking."

He pistoned in and out of her snug pussy slowly at first until her juices thoroughly coated his cock. He picked up the pace, thrusting inside her as hard as he could. She felt amazing. Perfect. As if she were made just for him. *Mine.*

Leah moaned and pushed against the wall trying to draw him deeper inside her hot, greedy cunt. She clenched her pussy muscles, gripping him even tighter. He was close. "So good, Leah."

He reached down between them and rubbed her engorged clit while he continued fucking her for all he was worth.

"Oh Heath, I'm going to come."

He felt his spine tingle and his balls draw tight. "Come for me, Leah." His thrusts became erratic, and he saw stars as he emptied his balls deep inside Leah's waiting pussy. She clung to him, shouted his name, and followed him over.

He was proud he could make his woman scream like that. Right or wrong, good thing or disaster, Leah was his and only his.

It wasn't until he'd given her his last drop of cum and was coming back down from the best orgasm he'd ever had that he realized in his hurry to get inside her, he'd forgotten a condom. *Shit.*

Heath waited for panic to set in, but it didn't. That was fucked up. Or maybe it wasn't. Just for a second he allowed himself to imagine what it would be like for Leah to be pregnant with his child before he untangled her legs from around his waist and gently set her down on her fuck-me heels. He wasn't opposed to the idea. Quite the opposite.

Now's not the time for babies. Slow the fuck

down.

Leah appeared flushed and sated. She looked at him with such love and emotion his heart fluttered in his chest. He was at a loss. Totally out of his depth but knew he didn't want to be anywhere else.

She let go of her dress skirt, and it fell back down into place. He preferred seeing her flesh. She giggled. It was music to his ears. "Wow," she whispered.

He kissed her warm forehead. "Wow indeed. Can you get yourself into bed? I'll be right in."

She nodded, and although she was a little wobbly, she slowly made her way to the luxury suite's bedroom. Heath padded to the plush bathroom to clean up and get his head on straight. Luke had spared no expense in reserving the best suites the Fairchild Hotel had to offer. Even the bathroom was over the top.

Heated white Italian marble floors warmed his socked feet as he walked to the vanity. A white jetted tub was conveniently placed in one corner of the oversized room. The ceiling dripped with glistening chandeliers and a six-foot plush, white backless couch sat in front of a huge glass enclosed shower with a multitude of shower and steam heads.

He couldn't help but laugh when he looked at himself in the vanity mirror. His hair was a mess from Leah's tugging. That stupid top hat had fallen off again. He was naked from the waist down except for his socks and still had his tuxedo vest, shirt and bowtie on.

"What the fuck are you doing?" he muttered to himself. He sighed and shook his head. "Claiming my woman, that's what."

That was the truth, regardless of how conflicted he felt about it. He should walk away. Let Leah find a man who was better for her. Who had his shit together physically as well as emotionally. Who was perfect, like her.

But now that he'd had a taste of her, he couldn't let her go. If that made him a selfish bastard, so be it. He'd stick around as long she wanted him to and hoped he survived when she eventually moved on.

Unless she was pregnant. Then they'd be linked for life. *Shit.* As much as Heath wanted her, he didn't want her with him out of obligation. He wanted her with him because she *wanted* to be there. What were the odds he'd just gotten her pregnant anyway? He had no way of knowing. And wouldn't *that* go over well with Jake and Leah's father? *Fuck.*

He took a deep breath and tried to calm down. There was no sense getting upset unless there was something to get upset over. He removed the rest of his clothes and cleaned up. Before joining Leah in the bedroom with a damp washcloth he took a good look at himself in the mirror.

He suspected she would be turned on by his many tattoos including Semper Fi on his left forearm and the barbed wire around his right bicep, just like many of the brothers in his Marine unit wore in a show of unity. He wasn't sure how she'd react to the battle scars scattered on his upper torso, back, and thighs. Old insecurities nearly stopped him from joining her in the bedroom. His need for her won out in the end.

Heath stopped dead in his tracks at the sight before him in the bedroom. Leah was lounging in the center of the king size bed sitting up with her back against the headboard, wearing the top hat and a sultry smile. The white sheets were bunched up at her waist exposing her full, lush tits and pebbled, dusky pink nipples. His cock immediately got hard, and his mouth watered. Did she realize how gorgeous she was?

He knew he didn't deserve the goddess before

him, not by a long shot. And he didn't give a shit. He would take what she offered as long as she was willing to give it.

"I thought you forgot about me," she purred.

He stroked his cock as he walked to the bed and sat down beside her. He leaned over and took a tempting nipple in his mouth, laving and sucking until she moaned and squirmed. He released the taut bud and smiled at his woman. It did wonders for his ego to see the disappointed expression on her face. He'd pleased her, and that made him feel like the millions or more Luke was worth.

"I could never forget about you." Heath went to pull the sheets down so he could clean her up but she tried to stop him.

"You don't have to. I'm not exactly model thin." Leah frowned, and it hurt his heart to know she didn't understand how beautiful she was.

"Thank fuck for that. You're perfect just the way you are." He moved her hands away and pulled the sheet down. The sight of his cum dripping out of her pussy had his cock aching. He shook his head and wiped her clean. "I'm sorry I was so caught up I didn't use a condom, Leah. I'm always careful, and I'd never do anything to hurt you."

"I know. I was caught up, too. It'll be okay." She reached underneath the pillows behind her back and pulled out a strip with three condoms. "We can use these next time."

He tossed the washcloth aside and positioned himself beside her. He hoped she was all right. She didn't seem upset, so he'd follow her lead. He tore a condom packet from the strip and quickly sheathed his cock, needing to be inside her again.

"Let's use one now. Come up here and ride me."

With his help, Leah straddled him. She was the most exquisite thing he'd ever laid eyes on. "Is the top hat a new look for you?" he teased as she slowly impaled herself on his aching dick. Her pussy was so snug, so incredibly perfect. He was one lucky son of a bitch.

Leah leaned her head back and moaned as her tight cunt gradually adjusted to his cock. He held on to her full hips, keeping her steady. She smiled down sexily at him and shrugged.

"I thought why not? Why should the men have all the fun?"

His woman wanted to have some fun? He was more than happy to oblidge. He lifted her up and slammed her back down on his rock-hard dick, and they both moaned. "Come on, Leah, ride me hard. Let's have some *real* fun."

She nodded. "Mmm…" She rode him in earnest, her luscious tits bouncing each time she slammed down on his cock. He would never get the image out of his mind. He leaned forward, grabbing the mouthwatering mounds and sucking one hard nipple while pulling on the other.

"Oh, Heath," Leah groaned as she rode him faster and harder. Heath's hips thrust up, adding more friction. Her pussy was so tight it was strangling his needy dick. He was close.

He surprised her and moved her so he was on top of her. The top hat fell off and rolled off the bed onto the floor. He continued to thurst in and out of her over and over. He'd never get enough. How could he?

She wrapped her legs around his waist and held him tight. "I'm going to come."

He reached between them and rubbed her little clit, causing her to moan so loudly they probably heard her in the next room. Her pussy choked his dick as she came, and he followed her over filling the condom with so much cum he thought some might leak out.

Vowing to be more cautious, he carefully pulled out of her convulsing pussy, holding on to the condom, and lay down beside her, both of them gasping for air. She snuggled up against him and put her head on his chest. He gently stroked her thick, silky hair, feeling like everything in his life was perfect instead of dark and broken.

She lazily stroked his chest, grazing over some of his scars.

"I'm sorry I have so many scars. I hope it doesn't bother you." He wished he didn't feel self-concious, but he did. It was just another reason he thought she should be with someone else.

She looked up at him with a surprised experssion on her beautiful face. "I'm not bothered. Not in the way you think. Just the fact you were hurt at all. That's what bothers me. I happen to think you're pretty hot." She placed her head back on his chest and then surprised him by kissing the scars she could see.

Tears pricked his eyes. What had he done to deserve the woman in his arms? He had no fucking clue but would revel in her as long as he could.

A while later, after using the other two condoms, Heath was wrapped around Leah, fighting to stay awake. When he was this tired, he normally didn't have combat nightmares. He sighed and kissed her shoulder. "I don't usually sleep with my hearing aids in, and you've wiped me out."

He felt and heard her chuckle. "It's okay. I understand. You wiped me out, too, stud."

This time *he* chuckled. *Stud.* Christ, she was adorable. If it weren't for the family brunch, he'd just as soon they stay in bed all day Sunday. They'd agreed not to linger too long at brunch so they could get back to Leah's room as soon as they could.

Heath untangled himself from her and missed the feel of her soft warm skin. The feel, taste, and scent of her were addictive. He quickly removed his hearing aids and wrapped himself around her again, settling in to sleep. He hoped for a nightmare-free sleep. He didn't know how she'd react if she witnessed him having one of his horrific combat nightmares. It would be best for her if they didn't go past the weekend, so she'd never have to.

She must have assumed that without his hearing aids he wouldn't be able to hear her. But he heard the faintest of whispers floating through the air as she relaxed in his arms and fell asleep.

I love you, too, Leah.

****

Leah startled awake as Heath's cell phone alarm blared to life. She felt him stir and heard him curse under his breath. She turned around and watched him turn over and shut the alarm off. He slipped his hearing aids in place and reached for her. She happily snuggled close. She'd never slept better, wrapped in his warm, strong body.

They lay together in comfortable silence. She was beyond thrilled with how the evening or early morning had turned out. If she'd ever doubted their physical compatibility, those fears had been put to rest. She was sore all over, in the best of ways, but she'd never felt better. Never felt more like a woman than she did after being with the love of her life.

Leah wasn't the most sexually experienced woman in the world, having only two previous lovers, if you could call idiot college boys lovers. She believed she and Heath were amazing in bed together. She also believed she'd pleased him as much as he'd pleased her.

And shit, did he know how to fuck. And eat pussy, which had been a first for her. She'd had no idea what she'd been missing.

If she could change one thing about the evening it would have been not whispering to her warrior that she loved him as she fell asleep. She knew he hadn't heard her since he'd taken out his hearing aids, but she didn't want to spook him. She hoped he'd want to continue their intimate relationship beyond the weekend, but she needed to be careful. She'd enjoy their time together for however long it lasted. It was all she could do for now.

Heath kissed her forehead and held her tight. She could get used to waking up like this *every* morning.

Slow down. One step at a time. Don't scare Heath away by seeming needy.

"Are you doing all right? Are you sore? I should have let you get more rest, but I had to have you. I know it's not an excuse," he said and lovingly stroked her hair.

She leaned up on her elbow, looking into his troubled eyes. How could he be even more gorgeous with his hair mussed up from sex and sleep and his jaw covered in dark blond stubble?

"Stop apologizing. I'm sore, but it's all right. I wanted you, too." She gently kissed his warm lips and sat up. *Shit.* She stretched a little, loosening the kinks in her back and neck. There was time for a quick bath in the jetted tub. Maybe Heath would join her.

Much to her disappointment, Heath got out of bed and began dressing. Now that she'd seen him naked, she preferred him that way. She admired him as he got ready to leave with the sheets bunched up at her waist and her breasts exposed. Even her nipples were sore. Her man liked her breasts. She wasn't about to complain.

After he dressed and was holding his jacket, he sat down beside her. "Why don't you take a bath?

There's plenty of time."

She took one of his large hands in hers. So warm, powerful, and strong. "I was hoping you'd join me, but you seem to be in a rush to leave." She hoped she didn't sound whiny. She just wanted more of him, any way she could get him.

He kissed her gently and smiled. Her stomach did that fluttery thing it always did when he smiled at her.

"If I did that, we'd never make it to brunch, and we all promised we'd be there."

Her stomach growled at the mention of food. She supposed getting something to eat wasn't a bad idea. She'd certainly worked up an appetite. She imagined he had, too.

"When you're finished and ready to go, come to my room and we'll go down together, okay?"

She nodded. She could do that. Not be clingy and relax in the tub before joining him to eat with the rest of the family. "Sure."

"Good." Heath kissed her again and stood. "I've changed my mind about our arrangement for the weekend."

No! She tried not to appear upset, but her stomach twisted up in knots. Heath wanted to cut the weekend short? This was it? One night together was all he wanted? Why bother with brunch? She should head home instead. How could she act like everything was fine when inside her heart was breaking?

"I want us to continue on after today. I'd like to take you on a date this coming Friday. What do you think?" Heath waited for her answer with an expectant look on his rugged face. Did he think she'd turn him down?

Hell yes! It sounded fantastic to her. She took a deep breath and calmly nodded when what she wanted to do was jump up for joy and do cartwheels in her fancy hotel suite.

"I'd like that a lot." There. That sounded calm and cool.

Relax. It's just one date.

He looked relieved and nodded. "Good. Where would you like to go? Dinner?"

A dinner date with her man. And Heath was hers, even if he was slow coming to that conclusion. She was so thrilled it was killing her to play calm, cool, and collected. She knew where she wanted to go on Friday.

"Cassie raved about Golden Horns. Can you ask Luke to get us a table?" She couldn't imagine Luke refusing since he'd already helped Cassie and Jake get one during the restaurant's soft opening.

While the ladies got ready for the wedding, Cassie had informed them about Envy Entertainment's expansion in Chicago. Kyle Asher from Envy, Texas, was bringing his family of companies to Chicagoland. They included Golden Horns Steak and Char House, Impulse, a lingerie and adult toy shop owned by former super model Heather Bellatoni, kinky BDSM club, Club Envidious, and a ladies' erotic book and social club, the Twisted Tea Society, where the men served the women refreshments, gave them foot and shoulder rubs, wearing nothing but a bowtie. It was wild!

He shook his head and flashed her a sly grin. "I don't need to call Luke. Kyle Asher's a friend of mine. So is his younger sister, Grace. I'll call him myself and reserve us a table for Friday."

Leah's mouth fell open. He was friends with the big bad southern Dom and kinky entrepreneur? "How do you know him?"

He chuckled and walked out of the bedroom. "We'll tell you all about it on Friday. Take your bath. I'll be waiting."

As soon as she heard her suite door close, she got out of bed. Her sore muscles protested and prevented her from racing to the bathroom. Heath was right. She needed a hot soak.

She padded to the suite's luxurious bathroom with a smile on her face. Things were definitely looking up. Her stomach let out an angry growl.

"First a bath, then food, then more Heath." Leah couldn't help it. She felt optimistic about the future. She couldn't believe Heath knew Kyle Asher. She wondered what other secrets he might be hiding.

• Chapter Five

It was Friday night, and Leah was still reeling over the revelations from Jake and Cassie's wedding brunch last Sunday. The most serious had been Darren Stryker's stage 1B exocrine pancreatic cancer diagnosis.

Darren was Luke's uncle and had become his guardian after his parents died in a car wreck when Luke was ten. Darren had also been the Chicago Cobras' owner until Monday when during a press conference at Cobras' headquarters he'd stepped down, turning ownership of the entire baseball organization, their children's foundation, and their family's real estate business to Luke. Luke had retired from the team to assume his new responsibilities.

At the beginning of the press conference Brenna Sinclair, actress extraordinaire, had apologized for lying to the public about her romantic relationship with Luke. In reality they had only been friends, and Brenna came out as bisexual. Setting the record straight was the least she could do after the paparazzi nightmare she'd generated at the Fairchild Hotel after they had all finished eating brunch.

Sadly, the five-year survival rate for Darren's cancer was only about twelve percent. He'd successfully undergone surgery to remove the cancerous tumor that Tuesday morning and had been in the hospital since.

On a happier note, Luke and Abbey had gotten engaged, having reconciled their issues. They were getting married on Labor Day, and Leah had been asked to be a bridesmaid and Heath a groomsman.

It was about thirty minutes before Heath was due to pick her up for their first official date, and she was still undecided about what to wear. She was nervous and wanted to choose correctly since she was meeting Kyle Asher and his sister, Grace. She didn't want to embarrass Heath in front of his friends.

With the help of her new sister-in-law Cassie via texted pictures and their current cellphone call on speaker, she was down to two dresses. Both lay on her bed in wait for a final decision.

She put her hands on her hips and sighed. "Ok, Cassie, what's the verdict? Which dress should I wear? It's crunch time. Heath will be here in half an hour," Leah said to her cell phone on her bed next to the dresses up for consideration.

"I'm thinking the forming fitting black and flowered dress with the V-neck and sexy asymmetrical hemline," Cassie suggested.

Leah liked the dress a lot. It was new, but she wasn't sure about the hemline for this date. It started at about mid-calf on the right side, angling up and ending about two inches above her left knee. It was form fitting but not tight and figure flattering.

"I know you think it might not be conservative enough to meet Kyle and Grace, but that hemline is fun and flirty, not sleazy. Not to mention, the man owns kink clubs. He's around *naked* people all the time," Cassie reminded her. "You'll be over-dressed," she teased.

Leah laughed at that. She'd hardly be over-dressed. "Golden Horns is a high-end steak house, not a kink club, and you know it. But you're right, I'm going with fun and flirty. Thanks."

They said their goodbyes, and she quickly got dressed. Heath was punctual to a fault, which didn't leave her much time to spare. She'd just spritzed herself with Vanilla Musk when her unit's buzzer rang.

"Right on time." Leah nearly floated to her front door and pressed the intercom/access button. "Hello."

Leah blew out a breath hoping it would slow her racing heart.

"Hey, babe. It's me." *Babe*. He was calling her "babe" now, instead of "little girl". He'd acknowledged after the brunch drama had come to its climactic conclusion he no longer saw her as a little girl, but a woman. Finally!

"Hi. Should I come down?" Leah was ready to get the evening started. Her stomach growled on cue.

"Buzz me in." Heath's curt reply threw her. Had he changed his mind about their date?

She paced, waiting for Heath to arrive at her door, her stomach in knots. Something was wrong, but she didn't know what. The week had been stressful since the shocking revelations were divulged after brunch, but the family was dealing with them the best they could.

The work week had been somber as expected but also sexy where Heath was concerned. Stolen kisses and groping during some rare private moments at the office had left her achy and needy. They hadn't seen each other outside the office all week.

She unlocked and threw the door open as soon as Heath knocked. If he was going to tell her he'd changed his mind about pursuing a relationship with her, she wanted to know now. Did he have to dump her looking so handsome in his navy-blue dress pants and crisp white shirt rolled up to the elbows exposing the sexy Semper Fi tattoo on his left forearm? *Damn him.*

Heath frowned at her, and she knew this was it. "You just open your door without checking the peephole first? What the hell?"

"I knew it was you."

Heath shook his head disapprovingly in the hallway and sighed. "You didn't know since you didn't check. You knew I was on my way up, but didn't know it was me knocking."

Technically he was right, but why start an argument when he was just going to cancel their date anyway?

"Just get it over with, please," Leah implored him.

"Damn, babe, aren't you the impatient one? Can't I at least come inside to give you your gifts?"

Heath brought her gifts? To break their date? It was then she noticed he had what looked like flowers wrapped in tissue and a bag from the Fairchild Hotel spa in his hands. She stepped aside, and he strode in.

"You brought me gifts?" Leah was confused. What was going on?

Heath shot her a curious look and nodded. "I didn't want the stuff from the spa and the flowers sitting in a warm car. That's why I wanted to come up, so you can put the flowers in water." He kissed her cheek and presented her with a dozen roses, six red and six white and the spa bag.

She hadn't expected that. "No one's ever given me flowers before. I mean, date flowers." She'd received flowers from Jake and her parents, but never from a man. It was silly, but she wanted to cry. He was so sweet. Their new relationship would take some getting used to.

He frowned at her and shook his head. "Do you have a vase?"

She nodded and took her gifts to the kitchen. Esther Myrick, her landlord, had updated the kitchen just before she had moved in, with warm maple cabinets, stainless steel appliances, and granite counter tops. The kitchen had a breakfast bar with three stools and a small dining area behind it with a table and four chairs. It was perfect for her and a few guests.

She reached into the cabinet under the sink and

retrieved a pretty crystal vase her parents had given her. After she had the stems trimmed and the flowers and baby's breath arranged to her satisfaction, she brought the filled vase to the living room and placed it on the center of the table in front of her couch. Heath was right behind her with the spa bag in his hand.

"These are beautiful. Thank you." She kissed him softly, but it was enough to warm her all over and rev up her pulse.

"I'm glad you like them. Here. I got you a set of the vanilla spa products that were in your bathroom at the Fairchild Hotel." He handed her the spa bag.

She couldn't believe Heath had gone to so much trouble for her. It wasn't necessary, but she was thrilled and touched by his thoughtfulness. She loved anything vanilla scented. It was her signature scent.

She had taken the hotel toiletries home. Now because of Heath, she had the full-sized versions to pamper herself with.

"Thank you for this." She put the bag down next to her beautiful bouquet and hugged him tight, feeling his erection against her stomach. "You know, we could order in instead of going out."

He cupped her ass and squeezed her flesh. Her nipples pebbled, and her pussy clenched. She'd rather stay in. After the sex-filled weekend they'd shared and their sexless week, she was so needy she couldn't stand it. Her stomach growled reminding her she was hungry *and* horny.

"That's tempting, but Kyle and Grace are expecting us. Not to mention you're hungry. I am, too. If you're a good girl maybe after dinner you'll be rewarded." Heath lightly spanked an ass cheek and headed toward her front door.

She tingled all over. That was unexpected. And

fun. If Heath and Kyle were friends, did that mean Heath was into BDSM? And if he was, she wasn't sure how she felt about that. She'd read erotic romance books with BDSM themes. Who hadn't? But books weren't reality, and her man was waiting for her with the front door open. She put thoughts of BDSM aside and grabbed her purse and keys.

Outside, near Heath's ingot silver metallic Lincoln MKZ, she waited in the warmth of the lovely June evening. She tried the door handle, but it was locked. He was right behind her. Why hadn't he used his key fob to unlock it?

She felt him at her back and immediately warmed up. He placed a firm hand on her hip. His car chirped, and the door locks disengaged. Before she could try the door handle again, Heath placed his large, powerful hand over hers.

"I'll open the door for you," Heath whispered seductively into her ear. She leaned back against him and felt his erection pressed against her ass. They should have ordered in and spent the night in bed.

She let him open the car door for her. It was also something no other date had ever done for her before.

"Just assume I'll always open the door for you, all right," he asked before closing her door and walking around to the driver's side. She made herself comfortable in the soft leather cappuccino colored seat.

"Haven't your other dates opened doors for you?" He buckled his seat belt and looked at her expectantly.

Leah quickly buckled up. "No. I'm capable of opening doors for myself, you know?" She wasn't sure why his question made her testy. Having her car door opened for her was thoughtful, but she didn't see the point in bringing up previous dates. The past was the past. She'd rather focus on the future. *Their* future.

Heath deftly maneuvered out of her complex and headed toward Golden Horns. "Of course you're capable. It's not about that. It's about respect, common courtesy, consideration."

She pondered that as they drove to the restaurant. She settled into her seat for the quick ride. Her little Cajun red Chevy Cruze was fun and sporty, but Heath's MKZ was all about luxury, style, and comfort. She decided she liked both.

She became increasingly nervous the closer they got to the restaurant. Although she was famished, butterflies had taken flight in her stomach and her palms were sweaty. She needed the evening to go well.

She saw this first date with Heath as a test. In her mind, it would determine if there would be others. And there was that little thing about meeting his friends, the Dom, Kyle Asher, and his sister, Grace.

Why did I suggest going to Golden Horns? It was too late to change their plans, so she had to do her best and not blow it.

Heath pulled into one of the few available parking spaces in the Golden Horns lot. So much for a soft opening. "It's crowded." When she reached for the car door handle, he arched a disapproving brow. She placed her hands in her lap and waited for him to come around and open her door.

Leah happily took his offered hand and exited the car. She could get used to this. It did things to her heart knowing he wanted to be respectful and considerate toward her. What a sad statement it was that she wasn't used to being treated better by the opposite sex, other than family.

He led her to the restaurant entry doors. She smiled at the two door handles. Each door had a steel half of a bull's head and horn, which matched the restaurant's signage.

Just before Heath pulled the horn door handle to open the door he whispered in her ear. "Did I mention you look delectable in that dress? I was so close to cancelling our dinner reservation."

She felt a jolt of excitement and stepped through the open door into the restaurant lobby and took a deep breath. *Game on.*

Done up in dark cherry wood tones, the lobby of Golden Horns held a wooden hostess stand to the left and several padded benches for waiting patrons to the right. Directly ahead was the lively lounge with what looked to be a dozen four seat tables, several booths along the windowed wall, and a dark cherry wood bar with seating for at least ten. Top shelf booze lined the shelves behind the bar, and two big screen televisions hung from the ceiling at each corner.

Although the hostess station wasn't occupied, there were waiting guests ahead of them. Two hunky bartenders noticed them and came right over with a stealthy grace she wouldn't have expected from such large men.

The big, burly bartender, wearing black slacks, vest, and a white dress shirt, reminded her of a blond lumberjack, complete with long hair past his shoulders and a neatly trimmed beard. A blonder Brock O'Hurn type who had to be well over six and a half feet tall. His dark-haired companion, identically dressed, was equally tall, with shorter hair and the most striking deep blue eyes she'd ever seen. They greeted Heath with man hugs and offered her friendly smiles.

"It's good to see you, brother. Who's your pretty friend?" the dark-haired bartender asked with a southern accent.

Heath wrapped his arm around her possessively.

"This is Leah Tyler, my date and my woman. Leah, mountain man over here is Brody Dobbs, and blue eyes is Keith Lanford. They came up from Envy with Kyle and Grace for the Chicago expansion of Envy Entertainment."

"Nice to meet you, Leah," Brody said.

"Welcome to Golden Horns. I'm heading to Envidious. I was helping Brody out before my shift," Keith explained.

By the time Keith left and Brody went back behind the bar, it was their turn to be seated. A knockout of a blonde bombshell in a form fitting baby blue dress that matched the color of her eyes and a welcoming smile, was at the hostess station.

When she noticed them, she smiled brightly and clapped her hands enthusiastically. "Heath!" Another southerner.

Heath smiled at the gorgeous blonde, and Leah doubted herself. How could she compete with this woman? Had he dated her before? Her previous hunger pangs were immediately replaced with a sinking feeling in her stomach.

"Babe, this is my good friend and Kyle Asher's younger sister, Grace. Grace, this is my Leah."

His Leah? She liked the sound of that. Her ego enjoyed a little boost.

Grace extended a hand, and Leah shook it, feeling more at ease. "It's so great to finally meet you, Leah. Dang, Heath. You said she was beautiful, but wow. And your dress. It's so fun. I've never seen anything like it."

Heath had told Grace he thought she was beautiful? And the gorgeous creature in front of her agreed? If that didn't make her feel ten feet tall, she didn't know what would.

Heath shrugged and winked at her. He took one

of her hands in his and gently kissed her knuckles. "What can I say, Grace? Leah's indescribable. Where's Kyle?"

Grace placed a hand over her heart. "Aww, aren't you sweet?" She grabbed two menus off a stack at the hostess station and led them to the main dining room. Diners sat around the room at dark wooden tables with high-backed cushioned chairs or in comfy looking booths around the perimeter of the space. Part of the kitchen was visible with its gleaming stainless-steel counter and prep areas. Leah noticed many of the female diners had their eyes on Heath. Not that she blamed them. He was an attractive man and at the moment, he was all hers.

Grace led them to a cozy booth in a semi-private corner of the dining room. It was perfect. It provided some level of privacy while still allowing for a nice view of the room, diners, and the kitchen. They sat down next to each other and Grace handed them their menus.

"Speak of the devil. There's Kyle," Grace said.

Leah looked up to see an attractive blond-haired man, well over six feet tall, broad shouldered, and dressed in a designer navy-blue suit walk to the center of the dining room. He was just as Cassie had described him.

"Hello, everyone. I wanted to take a minute to thank you for your help during our soft opening. I know some of you have dined with us multiple times, and we appreciate your patronage, patience, and feedback. You've made me, my baby sister Grace, and the entire staff feel welcome. I know kicking off Envy Entertainment's expansion in Chicago was the right decision, and it's because of *you* our grand opening tomorrow will be huge success. I'd like to offer everyone complimentary dessert and coffee this evening as a way of letting you know how much we appreciate you. Have a great evening, y'all."

Everyone in the room applauded. Leah's stomach did somersaults when Kyle approached their booth. She was going to meet a real live Dominant and BDSM club owner. *Holy crap.*

"What about Lauren?" Someone shouted just as Kyle reached their booth.

"Big sister is homebody, but don't worry. She'll be visiting soon," Kyle replied to the room.

"Do you *have* to call me your *baby* sister all the time?" Grace asked her older brother with a frown on her face.

"That's what you *are*, baby girl. Can you check with the kitchen and make sure we have enough for all the dessert orders we're going to get?" Kyle asked.

Grace rolled her eyes. "You should have thought of that before telling everyone they were getting free dessert. Leah, I hope we have a chance to talk before you and Heath leave. Enjoy your dinner." Grace left quickly heading toward the kitchen.

Kyle smiled at Leah, showing off slight dimples, perfect white teeth, and extended his paw of a hand. "It's nice to finally meet you, Leah. Welcome."

She shook Kyle's enormous hand and smiled back. "Thank you. It's nice to meet you and Grace. I'm looking forward to dinner—and dessert."

"Heath, how about Grace and I join you both for dessert?" Kyle asked.

Heath turned to her with a smirky grin on his handsome face. "What do you think?"

Leah knew she couldn't refuse, but she liked the idea of Kyle and Grace joining them after dinner. She liked Grace and was curious about the big Texas Dom and how he knew Heath. "That would be nice."

After Kyle left them and their server Jeremy brought them soft cheddar and warm pretzel rolls and went over the specials, she took on the challenge of Golden Horns' expansive menu. She was famished, and everything on the menu looked delicious. How was she supposed to choose one entrée?

Heath chuckled. "I know it's a huge menu. Pick something that looks good and we'll come back again so you can try something else."

Relieved and overjoyed he wanted to return with her, she decided on the filet which Cassie had recommended. After Jeremy left with their order, Heath pulled her closer beside him. Feeling him next to her heated her blood. She gulped down her ice water trying to cool down. They were in a room full of people for Pete's sake.

"All the attention you're getting is driving me crazy. Everyone's had their eye on you in your sexy dress," he whispered in her ear.

Her mouth fell open, and she quickly closed it. Was he serious? And jealous? "You've got to be kidding. All the women and a few men have been eyeing *you,* not me."

Heath shook his head and chuckled. "Not true. Don't you know how gorgeous you are, babe? The men and women who may have been looking at *me*, are jealous that you're here with me instead of them."

He cupped her cheek with his strong, warm hand and leaned in for a much too quick brush of his lips against hers. He thought she was gorgeous? She needed more than a quick peck and was about to take what she wanted when someone cleared their throat.

Startled and irritated, Leah pulled back, and Heath cursed under his breath. Jeremy stood in front of them with their dinner plates, looking embarrassed.

"Sorry, folks, but your dinner's ready." Jeremy placed their plates down, and Leah's mouth watered at the delectable aroma of her filet, Heath's beef tenderloin, and their sides of au gratin potatoes and mixed grilled vegetables.

Her stomach growled, and she giggled. "You're forgiven, Jeremy. Thank you. This looks and smells wonderful."

Heath nodded and smiled warmly at poor Jeremy. "Thank you, Jeremy. No need to be sorry."

Jeremy sighed, seemingly relieved. "I'll check on you in a little while. Enjoy."

They didn't hesitate and dug in after Jeremy left to check on other diners. She was pleasantly surprised at how delicious as her meal was considering how many popular steak houses were located in Chicago and the surrounding suburbs. She had little doubt Golden Horns' grand opening would go well. She made sure she left a little room for dessert. Heath didn't seem to mind she didn't eat like a rabbit, and she was grateful. *Another thing I love about him.*

Shortly after their table had been cleared, she noticed Kyle and Grace coming toward them. Kyle carried a large serving platter with a variety of desserts, plates, silverware, and napkins on it. Jeremy followed behind them with their to-go containers, a coffee carafe, Golden Horns logo coffee mugs, cream, and sugar. As anxious as she was for a taste of the tempting treats headed her way, she was more anxious to get the skinny on Heath's association with the big, bad Texan. She wanted to ask a million questions but knew she had to play it cool.

Except for Heath, who'd begged off, having eaten "too many carbs" at Jake and Cassie's wedding, they all settled in with their chosen desserts and coffee.

Heath took a sip of his black coffee and smiled at her. Her heart sped up, and she smiled back.

"I spoke with Darren today," Heath said to them all.

Kyle took a large bite of carrot cake and nodded. "How's he doing? Grace and I watched the press conference on Monday."

Grace frowned. "There was a lot of bad news during the press conference. We prayed over his surgery on Tuesday." She turned to Kyle and nodded.

"Luke called me from the hospital and put Darren on. Apparently, Darren was giving the hospital staff a hard time. He felt like he was well enough to go home." Heath shook his head and sighed.

Leah reached for his hand under their table and squeezed. "He's only days out of surgery. But that's a good sign if he wants to go home already. Not that he should though."

"I know. Luke wasn't able to reason with him so he called me. I told Darren to keep his ass in his damn hospital bed until his doctors told him otherwise or I would get Trace and some of my former unit brothers to keep it there for him."

Kyle shook his head and smiled. "Damn. You wouldn't need to wait on Trace and your unit brothers. I could round up Brody, Kevin, and some of the other DMs in ten minutes if you needed them."

Heath nodded. "Thanks, but Darren calmed the hell down after I read him the riot act."

"What's a DM?" Leah asked. She knew the acronym but couldn't remember from where.

"It stands for Dungeon Monitor, Leah. They watch out for everyone at Club Envidious," Grace answered softly.

Heath squeezed her hand and tingles ran up and down her spine. "I've DM'd for Club Envidious a few times, but not for quite a while," Heath admitted.

Leah's mouth fell open, stunned. He had been a Dungeon Monitor at Club Envidious? Screw trying to play it cool. She wanted answers.

"How do you know Kyle and Grace?"

• Chapter Six

Much to Leah's disappointment, Kyle and Grace busied themselves with their dessert while she waited for Heath to tell her … something. Obviously those two wouldn't be any help. *Thanks a lot, guys.*

Heath brought her hand to his lips and softly kissed her knuckles. Her body sizzled, but she gently pulled her hand away. She felt like crap when he frowned and seemed disappointed. She was, too. Enough with the secrets already.

He took a deep breath and nodded. "I've known Kyle and Grace since I was discharged. I stayed at Trace Baker's cattle ranch in Rapture, Texas, while I was recovering and trying to decide what I was going to do after the Marines. Trace was my Sergeant Major. Envy is Rapture's sister city, the next town over. The original Club Envidious and Golden Horns are located there."

Leah sighed. She'd been heartbroken when Heath chose to recover from his battle injuries so far from home. She and the rest of the family had wanted to help and support him, but instead he'd been secretive and distant. He had told none of them *where* in Texas he was. Mystery solved.

"I know all of you were upset, but I needed the time and distance. It was best for me at that time." Heath took her hand in his again, and this time she didn't pull away. She scooted over a little closer, feeling his warmth and strength, sharing the booth bench seat.

"How does being a DM fit into all of this? What do you do exactly? Just watch people have kinky sex?"

Grace, Kyle, and Heath chuckled, and her cheeks heated.

"There's no reason to be embarrassed," Grace

assured her.

"Heath, you mind me asking your girl what she knows about the lifestyle?" Kyle asked with a smirk on his face.

Grace rolled her eyes at her brother. "You just did! Very subtle. Leah, I'm so sorry about Kyle. Sometimes he's such a pain."

Heath kissed her cheek and glared at Kyle teasingly. "What *do* you know about the lifestyle, babe? Anything at all?"

Leah worried her bottom lip. She felt like an idiot as Heath, Grace, and Kyle waited for her answer. She didn't know shit. That was the bottom line. And the love of her life had been a Dungeon Monitor and who knew what else?

Although she felt anxious to learn this about Heath, she was also curious. Intrigued. Anything related to his world, she wanted to know.

She needed to tread carefully though. While they got ready for the wedding, Cassie had said not to reference anything *Fifty Shades* related.

"Only what I've read in romance e-books really." She shrugged, hoping she appeared nonchalant and that her answer didn't sound ridiculous or offend them. She was way out of her league.

Grace smiled wide and nodded enthusiastically. "Oh, some of the romances are so good. I especially like the paranormal ones."

Despite everything, Leah genuinely liked Grace. She hoped they could become friends. "I like those, too! Can you imagine a wolf, lion, or tiger shifter as your man? I loved the *Twilight* movies."

Grace took a sip of coffee and nodded. "If only."

Leah noticed Heath's and Kyle's amused expressions as she and Grace discussed their love of romance novels. Grace stuck her tongue out at Kyle.

Kyle rolled his eyes at Grace and shook his head. "Some of those books are researched very well, others not so much. So, back to reality. Heath was trained as a club Dominant and Dungeon Monitor back in Envy."

That answered *that* question. Heath had always seemed larger than life and "in charge" to her. Even when she was eight years old, his decision to join the Marines hadn't surprised her even though he had been a genius with numbers.

"In short, a DM ensures the club is a safe environment for our members to play in," Kyle explained.

That didn't tell her much. "Safe, sane, and consensual, right? Is that what you mean?"

Heath smiled proudly at her, and her heart soared. *Score one for me!*

"Very good, babe. So DMs make sure members follow club rules. We inspect the equipment to make sure it's working properly and that it's being used safely. We have to listen for trouble, make sure the club safewords are followed."

Oh! She knew this, too. "Red for stop, yellow for slow down, and green for everything's okay, right?"

Grace smiled approvingly at her and nodded. "Yes, those are the club safewords for public play. In private, they can be whatever the play partners agree to."

Heath continued. "That's right. And we don't really stand around watching people have sex. We don't linger. We keep moving around the play space. We're on the lookout for members who might be drunk or under the influence, even though the club has a two drink maximum and drugs are prohibited on the premises. We watch for overly aggressive voyeurs and other aggressive behaviors. Sometimes we're asked to escort a member to their car or perform first aid if there's an accident."

It all made sense to her. "So DMs are like BDSM cops and first responders?"

Kyle nodded and winked at her. "Exactly. Smart girl you have here, Heath."

But something occurred to her that made her heart ache a little for Heath. "Being a DM was another way for you to serve, wasn't it?"

He squeezed her hand and nodded. "Yes, I suppose it was. After I was discharged, the club training was a way for me to get some control back that I'd lost after getting hurt. I haven't done too much lifestyle-wise since coming back home from Texas." Heath glared at Kyle as if he were angry Kyle had mentioned his association with Club Envidious.

She understood. She could only imagine what it must have been like for him after getting injured. How frightening and painful it must have been.

Grace, as if sensing what Leah was feeling, spoke up. "Heath, I hope you don't mind me adding my two cents, but I remember what you were like when you first came to Rapture. Scared, angry, lost. I know all of you probably thought he should have recovered at home, but I believe the time away did Heath a world of good."

Heath brought Leah's hand to his lips and lovingly kissed it. Tears pricked her eyes. "Grace is right, babe. I needed to that time away from home. I'm sorry if it hurt you and everyone else. That wasn't my intention. Even now after all this time, I struggle. I get irritated, depressed, and short tempered sometimes."

"Like earlier when you got upset I didn't check the peephole before I opened my door?"

He chuckled and shook his head. "I *should* have been upset about that. I want you to be safe. I could have handled myself better though. That's what I mean."

He gently wiped away the stray tear that slid down her cheek. "I understand." And she did, but she still would have preferred him back home during his recovery. She sighed when he brushed his lips against hers.

"Why not bring Leah over to the club and show her around? I reserved you the Romantic Delights room for the night if you want it," Kyle suggested after fussing on his cell phone.

Grace frowned. "Maybe it would be better to bring Leah next Tuesday night instead?"

Leah bristled. She thought Grace liked her. Why didn't she want her to visit the club now? Granted she was nervous as hell, but she wanted to go. The Romantic Delights room, whatever it was, sounded promising. If Club Envidious was or had been a part of Heath's life, she wanted to be included. "Why is next Tuesday better?" she snapped.

Grace sighed and shook her head. "I'm sorry. It's not that I don't you to go. On Tuesday nights we host a masked open house from eight to ten. There's no play during the open house, and everyone is in street clothes. They wear masks and can tour the facilities. It's meant to be low-key and somewhat anonymous."

"Babe, it's up to you. You don't need to go at all. Not for me. Not tonight, next Tuesday night or any other time. I'm not really active in the club scene anymore," Heath assured her.

Leah was beyond curious, terrified but excited, too. "I'd like to go tonight."

****

Heath shut off the car engine in his space in Club Envidious's parking lot. It was a Friday night, and they were busy. He was going to kill Kyle for suggesting he bring Leah here. She hadn't said a word on the way over from the restaurant. They'd had such a nice evening until Kyle opened his big fucking mouth about the lifestyle and the club. *I shouldn't have brought Leah here. I'm not that involved with the club any longer, and this experience could scare her off.*

They both waved at Grace outside after she got out of her car and she sprinted inside the building. Kyle stayed behind at the restaurant so Grace could help him show Leah around the premises.

He sighed and shook his head. "Babe, you don't have to do this. It wasn't Kyle's place to butt in. He knows I don't have a lot of involvement with the club or the lifestyle that much anymore. Grace was right. Sometimes he's a real pain in the ass."

Leah furrowed her brows. "I like Kyle and Grace. Are you embarrassed to be seen with me inside the club?"

Shit. He took her hand and squeezed it tightly. How could she think that? "No, of course not. I'm proud to have you by my side. Never doubt that. I was going to wait a while to tell you about my association with the club. You don't need to feel pressured or rushed."

Hell, he'd only DM'd a few times in Texas and had played at the Chicago club but a couple of times. Mostly out of boredom, truth be told. And he'd ended up distracted with thoughts of Leah. *Fuck.* He wondered if Doreen was working tonight. He'd been ignoring her texts and calls since before Jake's wedding. She needed to set her sights on someone else to collar and marry her.

Leah's eyes glistened with unshed tears, and he felt like a total asshole.

"Did you think sex with me last weekend was boring? Is that why we haven't again since then?"

Boring? Fucking her, hell, just being with her last weekend had been the best experience he'd ever had with a woman—vanilla or kinky. Period.

"Boring? Not even close. How can you think that? I've been all over you at the office this week. I've never been so inappropriate in my life. The reason we haven't fucked again is because I was trying to build up anticipation. *Not* because I haven't wanted to get my hands on you."

Her smile soothed his soul. Heath prayed this little adventure didn't send her running. He'd have to make sure it didn't. He needed as much time with her before she decided he wasn't worth the trouble and eventually moved one. *Maybe she'll stay for good?*

Thinking in terms of forever with Leah was dangerous. He couldn't allow himself the luxury of believing they had a real future. Not with all of his issues.

Being with him wouldn't be easy. He should just drive her home and leave her alone. That would be the smart thing to do. The right thing to do. Except now that he'd had a taste of her, he couldn't. Not yet.

Leah nodded, seeming relieved. "Good. I know I don't really have a frame of reference other than books, and you're not heavily involved in the lifestyle that much anymore, but have you …done the sharing thing? I know it's none of my business, but I don't think I…"

He was going to fucking kill Kyle. Why couldn't the Texan mind his own damn business? He'd tell her whatever she wanted to know. There was no point in keeping secrets, and he didn't want to start their relationship off, regardless of how long it lasted, by keeping things from her.

Here goes. "Yes, back in Envy I did a few times. Kyle and I shared a woman. She was a server at the club. It was a first for me. I'd never done anything like that before. I haven't since then either. It's not really my thing, babe."

And wouldn't you know it Doreen *had* to come to Chicago to help get the new club up and running? Now that it was, she didn't seem to be in a rush to leave.

Leah blew out a breath and nodded. She offered him a slight smile. She must have thought he'd want to share her with some other man. That was never going to happen. She was *his* and his *alone* for as long as she wanted him.

"Let's go over the club protocols and what you should expect inside. You're required to sign non-disclosure and hold-harmless agreements. For your protection as well at the club's."

He opened his glove box and tossed his cell phone inside. "They don't allow cell phones or recording devices of any kind past the lobby. They can store your phone if you don't want to leave it in the car."

"I understand, thanks." Leah placed her cell phone in his glove box, and he promptly locked it. He reached into the backseat and picked up Jake's top hat. Maybe bringing it along would keep the mood light.

With the top hat on his head, Leah's hand tightly clasping his, Heath paused at the lobby doors of the Club Envidious facility and took a deep breath. *No turning back now.*

He kissed her forehead and smiled what he hoped was a reassuring smile. "Are you nervous?"

Leah nodded shyly.

"Babe, it's important that you answer with words, all right? Are you nervous?"

She nodded again. "Yes, a little."

That wasn't surprising. He was, too, but for different reasons. "Are you maybe a little excited, too?" He hoped she was. While they were together he wouldn't mind bringing her to the club or reserving one of the private themed rooms for them occasionally, if she were open to the idea.

"Maybe a little," she said and giggled. "I'm mostly curious."

What a relief. It would be all right. He *hoped* it would. He'd do his best to make sure it was. "We'll just treat this visit like an unmasked open house with the protocols. Grace will be with us, and we'll show you around. Ask all the questions you want. We can watch some scenes if any of them pique your interest. Then when you're ready, we'll go to the Romantic Delights room and we'll fuck all night to make up for this week. How does that sound?"

He'd almost rather skip the club tour and get to their room. He was aching to get inside her tight, hot pussy again. He wouldn't make the mistake of going so many days without fucking her again.

Leah smiled brightly and nodded enthusiastically. "That's a great plan."

He chuckled and opened the door. His stomach clenched when he saw Rocco seated behind the reception desk beside Grace. Shit, he'd forgotten Rocco worked club security a few nights a week and was a server for the club's Twisted Tea Society.

Grace stood up and smiled brightly. "I thought maybe you'd changed your mind, Leah."

Rocco raised a curious brow, and Heath shook his head slightly.

"No. Heath and I were going over a few things in the car. Hi, Rocco. I'm surprised to see you," Leah replied.

Grace placed the non-disclosure and hold-harmless agreements on the reception desk's granite counter top for Leah to sign. He looked on as she quickly read both documents and signed them.

"Welcome to Club Envidious. I work security part-time, and I'm a server for the Twisted Tea Society," Rocco informed Leah.

Her eyes widened. "I had no idea. That's great."

Great? Did she know about the Twisted Tea Society? *What the hell?*

"It might be good idea to get Leah one of the club collars as a precaution," Rocco suggested.

Grace came around the reception desk. "Good idea. I'll get her one for this visit."

"Thanks, Grace, let's not take any chances." He didn't want any misunderstandings during their visit. The club collar meant hands off.

"So, Leah, why don't I show you around the non-club side of the building first, including where we host the Twisted Tea Society get-togethers and the third-floor executive apartments and then we can tour the lounge, dungeon, and themed playrooms?" Grace's kind and welcoming disposition calmed Heath down considerably.

"That sounds nice. We learned about the Twisted Tea Society while we got ready for Jake's wedding. It sounds like so much fun."

Ah, that explained it. Did she want to join? He wasn't sure how he felt about that. Having a naked Rocco possibly serve his girl.

Grace's eyes widened, and she giggled. "You did? You should apply for membership! It would be wonderful to have a familiar face there. I'll get you an application."

Leah nodded enthusiastically and turned to him with such a sweet smile on her face, his heart did a little flutter in his chest. She kissed his cheek.

"You'll be okay here for a few minutes while Grace shows me around?"

"I'll be fine. I'll be right here when you've

finished."

He and Rocco watched Grace and Leah walk hand in hand through the key-card accessed door on the non-dungeon side of the building.

"What the fuck are you doing bringing Leah here on your first date?" Rocco admonished him from behind the reception desk. Heath sat down next to him, making himself comfortable. He may as well help sign members in while he waited on Leah and Grace.

"It wasn't my idea, all right? I wasn't even going to tell her about my association with the club for a while. I was most active in Envy while I was recovering, and not so much now. This is all Kyle and his big fucking mouth. It wasn't his place to say anything, but you know Kyle. He thinks he knows what's best for everyone."

Rocco grunted. "So you didn't say anything to Leah about me and my association? She was genuinely surprised to see me?"

He nodded. "It's not for me to tell her. You better not let Hannah anywhere near Kyle before you tell her."

Rocco shrugged and checked some members in. What was the problem with Hannah? The rest of them liked her. Believed she was a good match for him. After the club members entered the lounge Rocco turned back to him and pointed at the top hat.

"I thought it might lighten the mood for Leah. You *are* going to tell Hannah, aren't you?" He wasn't about to tell the Italian how to handle his business, but he didn't think lying was a good way to start their relationship.

"I'll have to see. I might not see her after Jake and Cassie's wedding gift reveal party on Sunday. So telling her might not be an issue."

Why was he talking like he and Hannah were over before they even got started? *Come on, man, what's the problem?*

"Have you spoken with her since the wedding?" Rocco had to give him *something*.

Rocco nodded and sighed. "We've been texting since the wedding. She's called a couple of times while she was waiting on deliveries or had time during an event."

"That's good, right? You like her, don't you?" Why did he look so conflicted?

"I do. I'm just not sure I'm the one for her."

Heath checked in a trio of members. When they were alone again he pressed. "Why not? We all thought the two of you were hitting it off at the wedding. Darren thinks the world of her."

Rocco pinched the bridge of his nose and closed his eyes briefly. "I know. I don't want to get ahead of myself. You of all people know it's not easy, right? You have more important things to worry about than Hannah and me right now though. Doreen's working tonight."

Heath's stomach knotted. "Fuck." Just his luck.

He didn't have time to contemplate how to navigate the pushy server and former play partner as Grace and Leah were back. Leah was wearing the club collar, a simple sterling silver chain with a Club Envidious engraved silver handcuff and key charm, indicating she wasn't available. He had to admit he liked seeing it on her. Her time with Grace must have gone well. She was all smiles. His heart did that fluttery thing again, and he felt his cock get hard. *Mine.*

He rounded the reception desk and claimed her lips. He'd rather take her to their room, saving the club tour for another time. He suspected she'd be disappointed, so he'd go along with their original plans and get her to their room as soon as she was ready.

"You ready for the *real* tour?" He brought her

hand to his lips and kissed her knuckles.

Her eyes dilated, and she blushed sweetly. "Yes, Sir."

• Chapter Seven

Leah'd had such a lovely time with Grace one-on-one. She liked the pretty southern belle and hoped they would become close friends. She was in awe of her after learning she'd joined the Asher family when she was twelve years old after running away from an abusive foster home in Tulsa.

Kyle had found Grace, beaten up, hungry, and frightened, rummaging through Envy's Club Envidious's dumpster looking for something to eat. After some patient coaxing on his and his older sister Lauren's part, they'd convinced her to let them help her and keep her safe. The bond forged between Grace and her new big brother had grown so strong that when he'd embarked on Envy Entertainment's expansion, she had enthusiastically followed him to Chicago.

Now Leah was being led by her new friend and Heath into Chicago's newest BDSM club. To say she was nervous would be an understatement. She couldn't help but feel excited and energized. Heath was sharing a part of his life that wasn't public knowledge. He trusted her, and that meant everything to her.

She held on to Heath's hand in what she hoped wasn't a death grip. Grace swiped her keycard over a scanner next to the door that led to the club's lounge. As it was darker than the lobby area, it took a moment for her eyes to adjust as they stepped inside.

Not surprisingly, it was a busy Friday night. Grace had done her best to prepare her for what she'd most likely see. For that she was grateful. She didn't want to embarrass herself, Grace, or Heath by looking like a deer caught in headlights.

The DJ's sensual, bass-heavy beats added an even

sexier vibe to the already provocative atmosphere. The lounge walls were painted a deep maroon, and overstuffed black leather couches were placed around the perimeter of the room. In the center of the lounge space about a dozen square tables that seated four in front of the crowded dance floor were being tended to by two female servers wearing black satin corsets with red piping and red bra cups with tiny black polka dots. The pretty, curvy, dark-haired server wearing the same club collar Leah had on, wore a black thong. The blonde server without a collar wore nothing but the corset and had her waxed pussy and bare ass on display.

Grace had shared servers could let club members look and touch if they weren't collared, and they were tipped generously in return. All interaction between servers and members was fully consensual. Leah didn't want to judge, but this cursory glimpse into the lifestyle was surreal. And sexy as hell.

"Can I interest you three in a Fruity Fuck?" Keith Lanford called out from behind the bar, similar to the one at Golden Horns. He was wearing a black leather vest and matching leather pants. Although he was tall, handsome, and exuded muscular sex appeal, he wasn't Heath. Even his tattoos, which showed a variety of jungle animals, didn't appeal to her like Heath's tattoos did.

Heath leaned in and whispered, "It's a drink, babe."

"Keith offers cocktails and shooters with dirty names Friday through Sunday. It's his thing," Grace said and shrugged.

The three of them took a seat at the last free padded barstools at the center of the bar with Leah seated between Heath and Grace.

"What's in it?" She'd never had a dirty-named drink before.

Keith waggled his brows and rubbed his hands conspiratorially. "So glad you asked. Aside from the vodka and fruit liqueurs, it also has OJ, pineapple, and lime juices. You'll like it. And they're on the house, from Leo and me."

Leah was confused. Who was Leo? She thought the bearded bartender's name was Brody.

"Thanks, Tony. Appreciate it." Heath kissed her cheek and put his arm around her waist possessively.

"Who's Leo? Why did you call Keith Tony?" Was it a kink thing?

Keith chuckled and shrugged. "Leo and Tony are just Brody's and my nicknames."

"He and Brody might have seemed friendly at Golden Horns, but don't let that fool you. They want to settle down, but I think they understand now that you're with me," Heath added and squeezed her ass.

Her heart swelled. She liked the sound of that. She could understand Keith and Brody. She wanted to settle down herself—with Heath. *Don't get ahead of yourself.*

Grace stood and looked over past the end of the bar. "I'm getting some food from the buffet. All I've had today was dessert with the two of you, it's been that busy. I'll be right back."

After Grace left in search of something to eat, Keith tended to two red headed female patrons. One wore a sheer black fishnet mini dress with nothing on underneath, and the other wore a fluorescent pink off the shoulder mesh fully ventilated mini dress with a matching G-string.

Although Leah wasn't interested in women sexually, she couldn't deny the spark of excitement as her nipples hardened. Hell, the lounge was filled with men and women in various stages of undress, with cocks, asses, tits, and pussies partially or fully uncovered. She'd made a concerted effort not to stare or be affected, but who *wouldn't* be aroused by such a titillating display?

On the other end of the spectrum she was surprised to see quite a few patrons in regular street clothes. Several of them sat enjoying buffet food and chatting with kinkily dressed patrons.

Keith placed their drinks down in front of them with great fanfare. "Two Fruity Fucks."

Leah laughed and look of sip of the pale orange concoction served in a tall Collins glass with a mint sprig garnish. Fruity and refreshing. "Keith, this is great."

Heath took a few sips of his drink and nodded. "She's right, this is good."

Keith beamed and smiled brightly. "Happy to be of service. Fruity Fucks are available all weekend." He stamped her and Heath's hands with a small red E. "We have a two drink maximum. This is the easiest way for us to keep track."

She nodded and took another sip of her drink.

Grace returned with two plates filled with an assortment of delicious looking food: chicken flatbread pizza, cheeseburger sliders, mini eggrolls, grilled and fried chicken tenders, and what looked like mini crispy cheese sticks. She slid the plate with both kinds of chicken tenders and cheeseburger sliders to Keith.

Keith's eyes widened, and he winked at Grace. "Thank you, darlin'. You read my mind." He popped a grilled chicken tender in his mouth and went to serve a patron wearing a navy-blue business suit.

"Does the lounge serve dinner?" Leah asked Grace.

Grace took a bite of her cheeseburger slider and moaned. "We call it an appetizer buffet, but we offer substantial food items. We noticed that many of the single members would stop by after work, have a drink and end up eating their supper from the buffet. We wanted to make sure it offered sustenance."

"The club took pity on us single members who didn't want to have dinner alone every night after work," Heath added.

Leah's heart ached. She hated the thought he might feel lonely. She would have happily had dinner with him anytime if she'd known he wanted company. Since she'd started living alone, she typically ate in front of the TV.

She and Heath people watched while they enjoyed their drinks and Grace ate her dinner. He took Leah's free hand in his and squeezed. Feeling less self-conscious now, she leaned into him and relaxed.

"Are you sure people don't mind us watching them?" The last thing she wanted to do was offend club members or embarrass him.

He chuckled and kissed her gently. Her body sizzled not only from his kiss but from watching a curvy, naked auburn-haired woman sensually swaying to the techno beat with her two strapping male companions, both shirtless and in tight black leather pants.

The man behind her held her arms up around his neck and was squeezing her tits and pulling on her nipples. The man in front of her was swaying to the music with his partners and had his hand between the woman's legs, stroking her glistening wet pussy. Leah watched, fascinated, as the men worked the woman over until she came on the dance floor surrounded by other dancers and interested spectators. Leah's own pussy pulsed and her heart raced when the man in front of the woman offered his pussy moistened fingers to the man behind her for a taste.

"Babe, club members are exhibitionists. They

wouldn't be here if they didn't want to be watched. Did it turn you on to watch those two make her come in front of everyone like that?"

Heath lightly sucked the pulse point on her neck, driving her crazy with need. "Yes, Sir," she breathed. Maybe they should skip the dungeon tour and head up the Romantic Delights room, right now. She needed to come in the worst way, but didn't want an audience watching.

Out of the corner of her eye spotted the blonde bottomless server shoot daggers in their direction. *What the hell?* Although the server was smiling as a seated club member was spanking her ass while another member seated at the same table was pumping two fingers in and out of her pussy, she didn't appear to be enjoying herself. Were the larger tips worth it if she took no pleasure from the attention?

She heard Heath curse under his breath and Grace suddenly stood up, her dinner plate now empty. "Heath, can I show Leah the ladies' room and then we'll take a tour of the dungeon before you go to your room?"

Heath stood up, finished his drink, and placed the empty glass on the bar, frowning. Leah followed suit. Was he upset? Did he know the server glaring at them?

"Good idea. Let's do that." He took her by the hand and led her out of the lounge into a cream-colored hallway, with Grace following closely behind.

He stopped in front of the door marked "Ladies" and took possession of her lips. His tongue wrestled with hers, and he ground his hard cock against her belly. Her head was swimming, and her legs wobbled by the time he ended his assault. Screw the dungeon tour.

"Don't take too long, ladies." He spanked an ass cheek and went through another door which she assumed was the dungeon. She was so aroused she nearly followed him.

Grace tugged on her arm and led her into the ladies' room. Leah stopped dead in her tracks once inside.

"Wow." This was nothing like the understated but elegant ladies' restroom on the other side of the building.

Grace smiled proudly as she glanced around the over-the-top plush bathroom. "We wanted the dungeon side bathrooms to be special. Especially for the ladies. It's still early, but sometimes members will just relax in here if they need to take a break from dancing or scenes."

She gazed around the enormous front area and agreed with Grace. This *was* special. Two long white marble counters housed four over-counter white sinks with large counter top mirrors, and lush red circular stuffed stools placed in front of each sink. The large space offered a variety of red plush backless couches, chairs, and chaise lounges. *Decadent.*

"Around to the right are the toilets and to the left are the left are the lockers and showers."

She went left past comfy red overstuffed chairs and chaises. Along a long wall were generously sized lockers with a line of backless red couches in front of them. She could see several shower stalls with three-quarter frosted glass doors etched with the Club Envidious logo—handcuffs and their slogan "It just seems kinky the first time"—at the end of the hallway.

"Showers?" She hadn't expected that.

"Some members participate in wax play. Some need to wash off lubes or lotions, sweat, or other bodily fluids," Grace explained.

That made sense. *If* and that was a *big* if, she ever played with Heath in the dungeon she imagined she'd want to clean up before leaving. Although she'd observed men and women of different shapes and sizes in the lounge enjoying themselves, she wasn't sure if she'd ever be that uninhibited herself.

She and Grace returned to the front of the bathroom just as the blonde bottomless server came storming in with a scowl on her face. The server pointed accusingly at her and glanced at Grace.

"Who the hell is this?" Another southern accent. The server put her hands on her hips and glared at Leah like she was ready to throw down.

"Who the hell are *you*?" Leah snapped before Grace could respond. Who *was* this bitch? And why did she have an issue with her? They didn't even know each other.

Grace went up to the server, stopping just inches away from her. "I'd watch myself if I were you, Doreen."

Leah didn't need Grace defending her. She could stick up for herself. Fuck Doreen and her bitchy attitude.

"I'm Master Heath's submissive, *that's* who I am." The server crossed her arms under her chest, nearly pushing her breasts out of her corset bra cups.

Grace shook her head and sighed. Leah didn't believe Doreen for a second. She wasn't wearing a collar for one. And she knew Heath well enough to know he wouldn't pursue a relationship with her if he were seeing someone else, kinky lifestyle or not.

"Oh really? Is that why you had some guy's fingers so far up your cooch he could have shaken hands with the man who was spanking you?" This bitch was crazy, and Leah was having none of it. But she obviously knew Heath.

Doreen was southern. Perhaps they knew each other from his time in Texas? That might explain why he'd seemed anxious to leave the lounge after witnessing Doreen's blatant display. She hoped like hell he wasn't jealous.

Grace sighed and shook her head. "Dang, girl. Don't lie like that. You were never Master Heath's submissive, and you know it. And you also know he's backed away from the lifestyle quite a bit since he left Envy."

Doreen frowned. She knew she'd been busted. "Well maybe I wasn't his sub, but we did have fun together back in Envy, a couple of times, at least."

Leah couldn't help but feel a little jealous. Being confronted by Heath's former lover or play partner wasn't high on her list of fun things to do. But she also felt sorry for the woman. It seemed like she still cared about Heath, and he was here with someone else. That had to hurt.

"My name is Leah, and I've known Heath—Master Heath my entire life. We're in an exclusive relationship." That was all she was willing to say. She wanted to get back to Heath and put this confrontation behind her.

Doreen's eyes widened. "*You're* Leah?"

Grace put her arm around Leah's shoulders and pulled her in tight. "That's right. This is Master Heath's Leah."

What? "Did he talk about me?"

Doreen snorted. "That's putting it mildly. All he ever did was talk about you. But that's the club collar you're wearing, not Master Heath's," Doreen pointed out.

She couldn't help but smile. Even when his world had turned upside down, Heath still thought about her and talked about her. That had to mean something. *Maybe he loves you.* She shouldn't get ahead of herself. She was here, and that was an important step.

Grace touched Doreen's shoulder in a comforting way. "That's because Kyle stuck his nose in their business and suggested they visit the club. This is Leah's first visit."

Leah stepped back giving Grace and Doreen their space. It felt like Grace had more to say.

"You've made it real obvious that you want to be collared and married, honey. So much so it seems needy and opportunistic. No one wants to feel like they're being used or they're a part of an agenda," Grace told Doreen, who looked close to tears. "You have to become the kind of person you want to attract and then it will happen. We've seen it happen in Envy, and we're already seeing it happen here."

Doreen nodded her head sadly. "You're right. I know I only came to Chicago to help get Club Envidious up and running, but I thought maybe I would stay if it's all the same to you and Master Kyle. I saw coming here as a fresh start."

Grace smiled warmly and nodded. "Me too. Honey, let me color your hair back to its natural beautiful brown—and you can get your fresh start started right. What do you say?"

Tears slid down Doreen's cheeks, and she hugged Grace tight. "I say yes. Thank you." She wiped her eyes and giggled. "I feel better already. I'm sorry, Leah. I don't want you to get the wrong impression of the club. It's a great group of people. In Envy and so far here in Chicago. Welcome."

****

Leah stood outside the dungeon door with Grace by her side. The butterflies in her stomach were darting around a hundred miles a minute. She'd made it through her first visit to the kinky lounge and the confrontation with Doreen. The dungeon was something entirely different. It was too late to change her mind. Heath was waiting for her.

As if sensing her nervousness, Grace squeezed her hand supportively. "It'll be fine. Like Doreen said, the members are great. Just make sure you address the Doms as 'Sir' or 'Master' and the Dommes as 'Mistress' or 'Ma'am'. When in doubt, just ask. There are Dungeon Monitors throughout the play space in case you get separated from Heath or me."

That was simple enough. "How do I address *you* once we're inside?"

Grace rolled her eyes and shook her head. "Thanks to Kyle, some members call me Gracie. I'm not a Domme, but out of professional courtesy a lot of members call me 'Ma'am'."

Leah took a deep breath as Grace opened the dungeon door. When the door clicked closed behind them, the sound of moans, cracking whips, and other implements being used to inflict pleasurable punishment greeted her. The heady scent of sex, sweat, and what she assumed were flavored lubes floated through the air.

She wasn't sure where to look—naked and nearly naked men and women occupied a multitude of equipment placed strategically around the vast play space in various stages of play and sex. Her nipples pebbled painfully and her pussy clenched. *Who would ever believe I'd be in a place like this?* The books she'd read didn't even compare to the reality of Club Envidious. *Amazing.*

She startled when Heath wrapped his arms around her from behind, lost in the sexual fantasyland that was Club Envidious. He ground his hard cock against her ass. She was relieved he seemed just as affected as she was.

"I was expecting you sooner, babe." He kissed the side of her neck. She closed her eyes and leaned back against him. His muscled strength pressing against her made her ache with need.

"Sorry, Sir. We had a little confrontation with Doreen in the ladies' room." She felt him stiffen behind her and regretted saying anything. It had all worked out. He didn't need to worry. "I promise everything is fine."

"Leah's right, Master Heath. There's no need to be upset. We handled it. Doreen won't be a problem," Grace assured Heath. A handsome Dungeon Monitor with wavy dark brown hair, a welcoming smile, wearing black leather pants and a black leather armband with the red letters "DM" stitched on it waved Grace over. He was observing scenes near several spanking benches.

"I'll leave you two alone to continue your evening. Master Heath, would it be all right if I hugged Leah goodbye?"

He squeezed Leah tight before letting her go. "Of course. Thank you for everything, Grace. We appreciate it." He kissed Grace on the cheek and gestured to them both.

Grace hugged her like they were old friends. "I'm so glad I got the chance to meet you. I'll call you soon."

She watched Grace walk toward the DM with a smile on her face. She'd enjoyed her time with Grace, even their skirmish with Doreen.

Heath took her hands in his and claimed her lips with the dungeon in full swing all around them. Breathless by the time he ended their kiss, she smiled up at him and giggled. He was still wearing Jake's black top hat.

"Don't laugh. I was offered some serious cash for this hat while I waited for you," he said.

She shook her head. "What is it about that hat, Sir?"

"I don't know, but I'm not giving it up. Come on, let's take a quick look around before I take you upstairs."

She was so on board with that idea. "Yes, Sir!"

As she held on to Heath's hand, he let her take the lead as to where she wanted to explore. The space was so large it was overwhelming. It didn't take long before she concluded it would require more visits to fully appreciate what Club Envidious had to offer. She steered clear of play areas where submissives were on the end of a whip she never wanted to be. She didn't see herself ever participating in that kind of play, even for Heath.

"See? Only marks from the whip's lash. No broken skin or bleeding," he pointed out.

She nodded, but still wasn't interested. "Yes, Sir."

Leah was drawn to a suspension station where two women were intricately tied up with brightly colored blue, pink, and purple ropes that resembled a kinky bathing suit with their erect nipples, glistening pussies and asses sexily exposed. From her reading she knew it must be Shibari. Both women seemed serene as they swung gently from the suspension apparatus. They didn't appear to be in pain. *Beautiful.* She wondered if Heath was skilled in Shibari.

"Master Gideon teaches Shibari classes if you're interested," the rope master's companion said to them. She was a stunning redhead tied in natural colored ropes that resembled a form fitting halter top bodycon dress that stopped at the knee.

"What do you think, babe," Heath asked.

Leah wasn't sure. What if the ropes burned or scraped her skin? "Does it hurt?" She hoped she didn't sound stupid.

Master Gideon's companion smiled warmly at her and handed her about six feet of red rope. It was surprisingly soft.

"We use and recommend hand-spun hemp, bamboo, or silk ropes. And you won't experience friction burns because the ropes aren't being pulled across your skin quickly. The ropes are tied tightly, so what you'll experience are compression marks when you're untied and those are only temporary."

"And sexy as hell," Heath added.

If that was the case, she could see herself bound in Heath's ropes if he were willing. She wanted to try suspension, too.

When Leah tried to hand the rope back to Master Gideon's companion, she waved her off. "Keep it to play with later."

Heath enthusiastically took the rope, and they said their goodbyes with him promising to contact Master Gideon about Shibari lessons. Leah couldn't wait. She wanted to see and feel his compression marks on her flesh.

They settled on watching scenes at the St. Andrew's cross stations. Or rather Leah watched. Some members were strapped or tied to the crosses. Some faced front, while others faced backward. Some were blindfolded or gagged. All of them appeared to thoroughly enjoy whatever pleasurable torture their Masters inflicted. She wondered what it would feel like to be blindfolded rather than just closing her eyes while Heath had his way with her. She shivered at the thought.

Watching the scintillating display sent waves of excitement through her, and she trembled. Instead of watching, Heath drove her crazy with need by grinding his hard dick against her ass, sucking on her neck, and kneading her breasts over her dress.

She shuddered in his arms, nearly coming standing there. "Sir? Can we go to our room now?" She felt him smile against her neck. Good, he wasn't opposed to leaving the dungeon.

In the blink of an eye, they were riding the

elevator to the second floor where the themed playrooms were. Heath had loosely wrapped the rope around her wrists for effect, and she felt ready to combust.

When the elevator doors opened he led her into the hallway. "We'll save the playroom tour for tomorrow. I have to get my hands on you. Now," he said as they reached the door marked "Romantic Delights".

She had no problem waiting until tomorrow for the playroom tour. She needed him desperately. The sooner the better.

But the top half of the door was a window with the curtain drawn open. That had Leah feeling nervous. Were others going to watch them together? Was that what Heath expected of her? As desperate as she was for him, she knew she wasn't comfortable being watched like club members were.

"It's *our* choice, babe. We can leave the door unlocked and the curtain open or we can lock everything down for complete privacy." Heath placed his hand on the door handle, waiting for her response.

Heath was leaving the choice up to her. She loved him all the more for it. He wouldn't force her to do something she was uncomfortable with. In time she might not feel self-conscious, but right now, she wanted privacy.

"Locked down, Sir."

She was rewarded with a sexy smile that made her ache. She'd wanted him so badly during the week. Leah couldn't wait much longer to get her hands on him.

As he led her inside their room by the loosely tied rope around her wrists, she welcomed the subtle scent of roses. She heard Heath close and lock the door but was distracted by the room itself—Romantic Delights. That was an understatement.

Done up in beautiful pink, green, and blue

pastels, the room was a romantic's dream. From the red and white rose petals sprinkled on the enormous four-poster bed to the huge jetted tub in the center of four roman styled columns set on a two-step platform. Real pink, red, and white flowers along with ivy were placed throughout the room. And so as not to forget they were in a BDSM club, Leah spotted the St. Andrew's cross in one corner, a bar suspended by chains near one side of the bed, and a leather sex swing on the other. Oh, Leah wanted to try that tonight.

She turned back to Heath after she heard him draw the door curtain closed with a smile on her face. "Did you have them sprinkle the rose petals on the bed that match the ones you gave me, Sir?"

Still wearing the top hat, he wrapped his arms around her and rubbed his thick, hard cock against her belly. Her pussy pulsed anticipating being filled by her Marine.

"That was probably Kyle's doing. I mentioned I was bringing you red and white roses. I hadn't planned on bringing you here tonight, remember?"

She wondered if he regretted it. She hoped he didn't. "And now that we're here, Sir?"

He let go of her, and her heart sank. *Damn it.* She had hoped their visit to Club Envidious would bring them closer, even though he'd stepped back from the lifestyle.

He unwrapped the red rope from her wrists and led her by the hand to the suspended bar at the side of the bed. Her heart raced as it seemed Heath wanted to stay after all.

"Now that we're here, locked up tight and in private, take off your clothes so I can inspect what belongs to me." Heath in "Dom" mode was such a turn-on she was practically shaking.

After he unzipped her dress she made quick work

of shedding her clothes. She desperately ached for Heath. She needed him badly. Now.

"Put your hands on the bar and spread your legs. We'll use the club safewords."

She placed her hands on the bar without hesitation, feeling the chill of the metal on her fingers. Vibrating with excitement, she wondered what the hell Heath was looking for in one of the nightstand drawers. He tossed a few condoms on the bed and approached her with a black blindfold.

Her nipples pebbled painfully, and she rubbed her thighs together, trying to relieve the ache. If he didn't fuck her soon she'd cry. Enough with trying to build anticipation.

He stood in front of her with the blindfold and shook his head. "I said spread your legs. Do I need to get the spreader bar?"

"No, Sir." She shook her head, spread her legs, and took a deep breath.

"I noticed your interest in the blindfolded members in the dungeon," he whispered as he tied the blindfold behind her head.

Her world suddenly went dark, but she simmered with excitement. The only drawback was she wouldn't be able to see Heath naked. She could hear the rustle of clothes. Probably Heath undressing. The scent of roses, mixed with their unique musks, drifted through the air.

She leaned into his hand when she felt him stroke her ass and yelped when he spanked it. She found she didn't mind the sting and basked in Heath's attention as he stroked her warmed flesh.

"What color are you?"

"Gr…green, Sir."

He spanked the other ass cheek, and she felt her arousal drip down her leg. She was on fire for him.

Ready to combust.

"Has anyone fucked this luscious ass, babe?" he asked on a sexy whisper.

She instantly clenched. She'd never had anal sex before. "No, Sir."

"We'll have to remedy that, won't we?" He was now in front of her. "I don't know which view I like better, the back or the front."

It did something to her heart knowing Heath liked how she looked. She knew it shouldn't matter. It was what's on the inside that mattered most, but she couldn't help feeling pleased he found her attractive. She believed Heath was beautiful inside and out.

When he skimmed her painfully hard nipples with his fingertips she shivered. More moisture flooded her pussy. She couldn't wait any longer. "Fuck me, Sir. I need you."

When he abruptly removed his hands from her body, she groaned. *Damn it.* She needed more contact, not less.

"I'm sure you must have read in your romance novels about topping from the bottom. I'll fuck you when I'm ready, and I'm not ready yet."

"Sorry, Sir. It's just that I want you so much. It's been almost a week." How could he have so much control? She was ready, beyond ready for him.

He chuckled and licked a nipple with his warm tongue. She gripped the bar tightly and swayed causing the chains to rattle. He laved at the tight bud enthusiastically until she nearly came standing there, then pulled away. *No!* She was so close.

"You don't get to come yet. I have to finish my inspection."

She inhaled deeply, trying to calm her racing heart. When he ran a finger along her wet slit she squirmed and groaned but didn't say a word. When it sounded like he was sucking his finger clean more juices flooded her pussy. He was torturing her. On purpose. That's what he was doing.

He lightly skimmed a finger across a scar on her right knee. She'd gotten it when she was five years old and was learning how to ride a bicycle. Jake hadn't wanted to be bothered teaching her how, but Heath had been patient and kind and taught her how to ride. When she'd fallen and hurt her knee, he'd bandaged her up and encouraged her to try again. And when she'd succeeded riding without training wheels for the first time, he'd cheered her on. He'd been her hero back then, long before he became a Marine.

"Such a courageous, determined little girl you were. And still are," he whispered and tenderly kissed her knee.

He picked her up by the waist, and she instinctively wrapped her legs around him and held him tight as he walked somewhere in their room. Being blindfolded added to the excitement she already felt.

He gently placed her down in what she believed was the leather sex swing. The leather and steel rivets felt cool against her warm skin. Being suspended and naked sent her pulse thundering in her chest.

"Don't move. Let me get you settled."

Heath placed her hands on the chains at the back of the chair, and she wrapped her fingers around them tightly. He gently placed her legs in the leather stirrups, leaving her completely open and vulnerable. More than she'd ever been with a man. And because she was with *him*, rather than feeling afraid, she felt energized and alive. And needy as hell. She felt him step away and gripped the chains tighter, making them rattle.

"Heath? Um … Sir?" Had he left? Was he

opening the door or pulling back the curtain so others could see them?

She heard a muffled sound like a door opening and closing from what seemed like a short distance way, then what sounded like a wrapper crinkle closer to where she lay in the chair.

"Just getting a condom, babe. Nothing to worry about. I'm right here."

He caressed her skin with his powerful hands from her thighs, to her hips, her torso, and her breasts. He tweaked each nipple, sending jolts of pleasure to her clit. Her pussy pulsed, needing to be filled.

"Please … Sir," she breathed.

"Please what, babe? Ask me nicely for what you want."

"Please fuck me, Sir." Leah would lose it if Heath made her wait much longer.

"Good girl," he whispered before thrusting inside her, her arousal making it easy though his hard cock felt snug once she was completely filled. "You feel so fucking good wrapped around my dick. Perfect."

She agreed and lost herself as he held on to the swing straps and used the swing's motion to piston in and out her so hard she was gasping for air. Suspended while being fucked by the love of her life was decadent, dirty, and like nothing she'd ever experienced before. Everything with Heath was a new and amazing experience. Why had he waited so long to be with her? So much wasted time they could never get back.

Just as she felt the beginnings of her orgasm take hold, he rubbed her clit lightly. She wouldn't last much longer if he kept that up.

"Come for me, Leah. *With* me, babe."

She squeezed her eyes shut even though she was blindfolded as her orgasm crashed through her. She saw stars behind her lids and shouted, "God, I love you, Heath!"

****

"Oh no," Leah cried and tore the blindfold off. With tears in her eyes, she struggled in the chair, presumably to get out of it.

Having Leah tell him she loved him as they both came had been amazing. Seeing her moments later upset about it, hurt his heart. Even though he wasn't sure where their relationship was headed, he didn't want her regretting that she loved him or telling him she did.

Reluctantly, he pulled out of her tight, warm heat and gently grabbed her arms to stop her from struggling. If she got hurt in her haste to get out of the chair, he'd never forgive himself.

"Relax and let me help you out of the chair so you don't hurt yourself. Then let me carry you to the bed, okay?"

With tears streaming down her cheeks, she nodded. He wouldn't correct her for not following protocol. She was upset enough and their scene was over. He quickly but carefully removed Leah's legs from the leather stirrups and carried her to the rose petal covered bed, gently placing her down on the center of the bed.

"I'm so sor…sorry, Sir," she cried.

Heath held her tight, rocking her gently, trying to calm her down. "Forget the protocols. It's just Leah and Heath now. Why are you sorry?"

"I'm sorry I said I love you." She whispered so softly he had trouble hearing her even with his hearing aids in.

"Because you don't love me? Is that why you're upset you said it?" He needed to man up and clear the air. Win, lose, or draw it was time to set the record straight. He moved away from her just enough so he could look into her sad, tearstained face.

"I do love you. I have for a long time, but I wasn't going to tell you. Not yet anyway. And don't worry, I don't expect you to say it back." She made to move, but Heath held her in place.

"That's a shame because I love you, too." The shocked expression on Leah's face was priceless, and he felt like an asshole for not telling her sooner. She deserved at least that much. "I should have said something sooner, but I wasn't sure, and I'm still not, about what's in the cards for us."

She reached up and cupped his cheek. He leaned into her hand, savoring her warmth.

"We said we would take things slow, right? One day at a time and we'll see where things go. I think we should stick to that plan."

Feeling relieved, like a ton of bricks had been lifted off his shoulders, he nodded. He could do that. Take things one day at a time. It was the only choice he had as he wasn't confident Leah would stay with him long-term. His physical and emotional challenges might prove too difficult for her. Hell, they were difficult for *him*.

"Agreed. Now that we've got that settled, I took a peek in the mini fridge before I put the condom on. Master Asher stocked it with chocolate covered strawberries and bite-sized pieces of the carrot cake and triple layer strawberry cake you liked so much at dinner. Want a little snack before round two on the St. Andrew's cross?"

Leah's smile was so bright his heart swelled. God, he loved her so much.

"Yes, Sir!"

• Chapter Eight

Leah gaped, open-mouthed as Heath navigated his car through the few streets that made up Paradise Oaks Country Club in Oak Brook, Illinois. It was one of the most exclusive gated communities in the area and where Luke and Abbey were calling home.

She was glad for them, having resolved their issues during Jake and Cassie's wedding weekend and surviving the chaos that followed the wedding brunch because of actress Brenna Sinclair. She was a bridesmaid along with Abbey's friend, Karla, and Cassie, Abbey's older sister, was the matron of honor.

This get-together, a week before Luke and Abbey's wedding, served as a combination housewarming and bachelor/bachelorette party. A rather low-key event, in part so Darren could attend, a little over two months post-surgery, and stay overnight.

Heath turned on to Tournament Drive, driving slowly to take it all in. "Holy shit." He looked at her briefly with a stunned expression on his face.

"I know," she replied. Holy shit was right. Paradise Oaks was like its own small town within the city of Oak Brook. With only one hundred home sites and homes ranging from six thousand to nearly twenty thousand square feet, the luxury gated community offered amenities including an award-winning golf course with an onsite restaurant/pub, a mini day spa, indoor and outdoor swimming pools, ponds, parks, walking trails and more. If *she* lived here, she would never want to venture outside the protected gates.

She spotted the "coach house" off to the side of the enormous pavered circular driveway, which was an additional two thousand square foot ranch home in the same architectural style as the main house, a white, palatial Mediterranean estate.

Heath came to a stop behind Jake's car and cut the engine. "Luke told me it was a little more than he and Abbey needed, but they couldn't pass up the great deal their realtor negotiated for them."

After he helped her out of his car and they each got their respective gifts for the bride and groom out of his back seat. Leah had found Abbey some sexy lingerie and sensual massage oils from former super model Heather Bellatoni's Impulse website, which was a member of Kyle Asher's Envy Entertainment's family of companies. Heath's contribution—high end booze. *Men.*

Feeling a little lightheaded, she leaned against his car and took some deep breaths. She wasn't sure what was wrong with her lately. She'd been *off.* No appetite, uncomfortable most of the time although she tried to hide it from Heath. And she'd gained a few pounds so her designer custom-made Bellatoni bridesmaid dress felt a little snug a week before the wedding.

Brushing off her discomfort as nerves, she stood beside Heath and took in the Stryker estate. It was gorgeous and looked like it belonged on a Mediterranean hilltop. "What did Luke tell you?"

Heath wrapped his arm around her waist, and she leaned in close, enjoying his strength and warmth. The last two months or so with him had been surreal. Sometimes she couldn't believe it wasn't all just a dream. The man she'd loved her entire life, loved her back. They were taking things "slow", but they were together. That's what mattered most.

They'd gotten into a routine of eating lunch together at the office a couple days a week.

Many nights were spent together either at his townhome or her condo. Their time together hadn't only been rainbows and puppies, however.

She'd never forget the first time she'd witnessed Heath wake up from one of his combat nightmares. Not knowing he didn't like being touched right after he woke up, she'd tried hugging and comforting him the best way she knew how. She'd learned she just needed to back off until Heath reoriented himself. And there were a few bouts where he'd needed to be alone, not because he was angry with her but because he needed the emotional space. Her soul ached for his continuing struggles.

They had visited Club Envidious a few more times. She'd been too shy to play in the dungeon, so they had reserved the Roman Times, Arabian Nights, and the Tropical Resort rooms. There were still a few more to try.

"Just that the previous owners were getting divorced and the husband was so desperate to get out he was flexible with price and included all furniture. He's got the basement set up like a man cave, and there's an outdoor kitchen with a gourmet grill."

Leah chuckled. Abbey had told her a little more than Luke's bare-boned explanation. "The owner's wife was cheating on him with a golf instructor and two caddies," Leah explained.

As she looked around she noticed the surveillance cameras. She'd bet Rocco and Dixon-Shaw Security had a hand in getting their security set up. She didn't envy Luke and Abbey in that regard. Now that Luke owned the entire Chicago Cobras organization, the children's foundation, and Stryker Real Estate Holdings outright, he could become a target. She hoped he and Abbey were and felt secure in Paradise Oaks.

"Damn. That explains why Luke had all the mattresses replaced. Poor guy."

"There are still empty lots available to build on,

but right now, this house is the largest in terms of square footage if you count the house and finished basement, about nineteen thousand square feet. And almost another two thousand for the coach house."

Leah couldn't imagine how Abbey was adjusting. Eleven bedrooms, eight en-suite bathrooms, four additional full bathrooms, five half baths, six fireplaces, a sunroom, professional kitchen with breakfast room, dining room, reception room, a library, elevator, intercom system and terraces and patios around the property. She knew there was more, but she couldn't remember it all.

"Did Abbey tell you Rocco's priest and Pastor Jenkins blessed the property before they moved in?" Heath took her by the hand and led her to the grand front entryway and rang the bell.

She smiled. Luke hadn't wanted to take any chances. He had insisted on having both a priest and a pastor bless the house. "Yes."

Luke led them from the magnificent two-story, white marbled foyer to the oversized great room where many guests were mingling. What she'd seen so far of the estate was amazing, and huge.

"Damn, Luke, you said we should just wear jeans, but I feel like I should have worn a tux," Heath teased and handed Luke the alcohol he brought.

Luke looked a little embarrassed and shrugged. "I know it's a lot, but this is our *home*, man. I've been wearing sweats or shorts since we moved in last week. Don't be a smart ass."

Heath laughed, and she made a beeline for Darren. He was standing with his companion Maureen and chatting with Abbey, Hannah Hailey, and Pam from HR. She greeted everyone, gave Abbey her gift bag, and hugged Darren tight.

"It's not the same without you at the office almost every day. How are you feeling?"

Two months into his recovery Darren seemed to be holding up as expected. He'd lost a little more hair since the last time she'd seen him and his complexion had dulled, but the fire in his blue eyes was still bright. Leah hoped and prayed for his full recovery even though the statistics were dismal.

"I'm doing well, dear," Darren replied as he hugged her back. "Don't count me out just yet."

She felt misty-eyed, and Abbey stepped in. "Now that everyone's here why don't we take a quick tour and we can get our parties started? The guys are going to hang out downstairs. They'll be plenty of pizza, booze, poker, and whatever else for them, and I thought it would be nice for us to use the sunroom. It's not as formal. I chose some tasty food from Cucina Antonetti's and Golden Horns for us."

The thought of food made Leah's stomach churn though she hadn't eaten much all day. She'd try to have a little something to eat as she liked both restaurants.

The pictures she'd seen of the rooms online didn't do the house justice. She agreed with Abbey that the estate was formal, but it was beautiful nonetheless. Abbey and Luke were planning on taking their time deciding which furnishings to keep and which to replace.

Leah's grandmother, Beverly, and Abbey's grandmother, Ruth, approached her as she sipped water while she gazed outside from the breakfast room. Her stomach felt somewhat settled, and she was a little hungry. Good signs to be sure. Both seniors had a gleam in their eyes and bright smiles.

"So, honey, how are things going with that sexy Marine of yours?" her Grandma Beverly asked, waggling her eyebrows.

"It's just us, give us the deets. That's how you say it, right?" Grandma Ruth asked her and Beverly.

She laughed at the pair. What a hoot they were. She knew she could trust them not to say anything with any "deets" she gave them. She wasn't sure however if she should mention anything about their time at Club Envidious or how proficient Heath had become with silk ropes. She enjoyed being bound and suspended very much. Knowing them, Ruth and Beverly would probably want to attend a Tuesday night masked open house at the club.

"Since Jake and Cassie's wedding, it's been amazing really. Sometimes I can't believe we're together, you know? But we're taking things slow. So far so good." She was ready to move things along a bit faster, but sensed Heath was still unsure about a long-term future for them. She didn't know how to make him understand that even with his challenges, she was with him for the long haul.

"I'm glad he finally got his shit together. The two of you should have gotten together sooner," her Grandma Beverly said.

"I know! Men can be so dense sometimes. And how are things between you two—intimately?" Grandma Ruth asked and winked.

Fucking amazing Leah wanted to tell them, but she refrained. "Really good in that department." The three of them shared a quick giggle.

As everyone headed to the second floor, Leah held on tight to Heath's hand. She felt optimistic that eventually they would host guests at *their* place. Either at his townhome or someplace they purchased together. *Things are going well. Don't push your luck trying to rush living together.*

****

The ladies were off at the other end of second floor in the master bedroom that was the size of Leah's condo as Heath stood in the spacious bedroom Luke and Abbey had deemed would be Darren's room. He was joined by Jake, Rocco, Luke, and the recovering patient himself.

Heath was still shaken up from the previous night's nightmare. This one had included Leah. And just like all the others he'd felt the same guilt and helplessness at not being able to save her from an IED blast that blew her to bits. In this dream her body parts littered the sand around him beside the others who'd also been killed in Sangin.

"Dad, you should just move in for fuck's sake. The master is at the other end of the hallway, so we'll all have our privacy. Even when kids come along. If you haven't noticed, the house is big. No, wait—what about the coach house?" Luke suggested.

Darren sighed and shook his head. "We've been over this. There's no reason for me to move in. There's no reason for you and Abbey not to take your three-week honeymoon at our new resort. It's important to me we don't change things more than we already have."

Luke shrugged, seemingly not convinced or willing to drop the subject just yet. "I know, but can't you understand why I, and Abbey, want you close?"

Heath understood. His own mother died in her sleep. He'd never gotten the opportunity to make the most of the time he had left with her. As much as no one in their family spoke openly about it since Darren's surgery, they all recognized that most likely they only had a limited amount of time left with him. And no one knew how much.

"I *am* close. I'm ten minutes away in Hinsdale, and my place downtown is down the street from yours.

Stop worrying." Darren placed a comforting hand on Luke's now healed shoulder, and Heath couldn't help but feel for the recently retired pitcher and his uncle/father. Luke's and Darren's lives had taken a significant and unexpected detour the last couple of months.

"Darren's right," Jake agreed.

"I agree. I know firsthand from back when my *nonna* and *nonno* were still with us," Rocco added. Heath knew Rocco had been raised by his grandparents after his mother left them when Rocco was six and his younger brother Massimo was three weeks old. Their piece of shit, drunk loser of a father wanted nothing to do with his sons and had disappeared after his wife left him. Five years ago, he'd crashed his car into a tree somewhere in Milwaukee, Wisconsin, drunk as shit and died on impact.

Luke quickly swiped a tear from his eye and nodded, relenting. "Promise me if things … take a turn, you'll move in with us. Please? So we can all be together. Can we agree on that at least?"

When Darren hugged Luke tight, Heath felt his eyes sting and watched on as Jake's and Rocco's eyes glistened.

"We can, and you have my word on that. Now why don't you tell the boys about our real estate expansion plans and the resort we just acquired?" Darren said after ending their hug.

Heath was all for changing the subject. Stryker Real Estate Holdings dealt with residential and commercial properties, not resorts or hotels that he was aware of.

Luke showed off his dimples with a smile and nodded. "Darren had mentioned taking Maureen to this private, exclusive luxury boutique resort in St. Lucia. Providence St. Lucia. It's on a private beach and has an award-winning spa and stunning villas and VIP suites."

"I got to know the owner of the resort during a few visits with Maureen. A good man, originally from New York, but up in age. When he decided to retire about month ago, he gave me call about a potential deal so I put him in touch with Luke since he's assumed ownership of Stryker Real Estate Holdings." Darren smiled and nodded to Luke.

Luke nodded. "We had a long but productive conversation about the property, and other hotels and resorts he owns in the US and overseas. The Providence St. Lucia is the first of his properties he's selling, and I think will be the first of many deals we do together. It's a high-end resort that celebrities, professional athletes, and wealthy clientele escape to when they need private down time."

Heath, Jake, and Rocco groaned with disappointment. If it was that exclusive and expensive, they'd never be able to afford taking their women there. Even if he couldn't afford Providence, Heath could still take Leah somewhere else—maybe Florida or Mexico.

"That's nice, guys, but it sort of leaves us out. We can't afford to take the women someplace like that. You know that, man," Jake said, speaking up for the three non-billionaires in the room.

Darren and Luke shared a knowing look. "Ah, but that's where you're wrong. We're making five of the villas that sleep up to four and have their own private pools permanently available for the family at no cost. Anytime."

Rocco's eyes widened. "No shit?"

Luke laughed. "No shit, buddy. Your complete stay is comped, the food, alcohol, excursions, and spa treatments for the ladies … and for you guys if you want them, not just the room. We're getting the family reservation process set up. I was told it should be ready in the next couple of weeks. Once it's in place, you can visit anytime you want."

Jake and Rocco quickly man hugged Luke and Darren, obviously excited. Heath shook his head, smiling. Leave it to Luke to include their family in their real estate expansion plans.

"I'm planning on the same type of arrangement for any other hotel or resort properties we acquire." Luke shrugged like it was no big deal he was offering them all free stays at luxury properties.

I wonder if the resort does destination weddings. Heath shook his head, not sure where *that* thought came from. It was too soon to contemplate destination weddings. If only he could be certain Leah was truly with him for the long haul. She'd already seen him at his worst over the last couple of months and stuck around. Could she do it long term? Would she *want* to? And should he ask her to? Would that be fair to her?

Regardless, as soon as the family's reservation process was complete he was taking Leah to Providence. With a spacious villa and private pool, they'd never have to get dressed or leave the villa if they didn't want to. And he looked forward to fucking her over and over again in their private pool.

Getting hard at the thought of a naked Leah at a luxury resort with him, Heath excused himself and set out to find her. The hallway was empty, and with ten other bedrooms to check he didn't know where to start.

In the third bedroom he checked he found Leah glancing out the window to the back of the estate and gardens. His heart swelled with love at the sight of her.

He wrapped his arms around her from behind and pressed his hard cock against her luscious ass. Although he hadn't taken her there yet, he had been preparing her. Maybe he'd take her virgin ass in St. Lucia.

She wiggled said ass against his painfully hard dick and giggled. He kissed the side of her neck and squeezed her ripe tits, feeling her nipples harden in his hands. She moaned and leaned back into him. He loved how responsive she always was with him. Shit, he loved *everything* about her. Period.

"I need you, babe," he whispered and unbuttoned her jeans.

She placed her hands on his, stopping him from pulling her zipper down. "What? Here? Now? Someone might come in."

Not wanting to embarrass his shy woman, he took Leah by the hand, led her to the expansive walk-in closet, and closed the door. He plunged his tongue inside her mouth, claiming what was his, their tongues dueling frantically until he thought he'd come in his pants.

"Take your clothes off, babe. We don't have a lot of time before we have to head downstairs."

Her eyes dilated and her skin was flushed. He felt pride knowing she wanted him as much as he wanted her. They rushed through undressing, and he rolled on a condom with shaking hands as he needed her so desperately.

He took her by the hand to a cushioned ivory chair in the corner of the closet and sat down, pulling her on to his lap. He devoured her mouth once more while stroking her wet slit. When he slipped a finger inside her tight pussy, she undulated her hips, letting him fuck her with it. When her pussy pulsed around his finger, his cock twitched painfully, wanting its turn inside her.

"Babe, I've got to have you. I can't wait." He pulled his throbbing cock away from his body enough so Leah could lower herself on top of him. He clenched his jaw as the amazing feeling of her hot, wet pussy made its journey until he was fully seated inside her.

"You feel so good," she whispered and began to slowly ride his dick.

Slow was not what he needed. She felt too damned good. He needed to lose himself in her. Fuck away his nightmare. Gripping her full hips, he guided her faster and harder up and down his cock. Her pussy strangled his dick, and her gorgeous tits bounced freely with tight, beaded nipples as she rode him. He was transfixed at the sight of his dick sliding in and out of her. He knew he wouldn't last long.

"I'm close, babe." He stroked her swollen little clit while she continued riding him for all she was worth. His balls drew up, and his spine tingled. He was on the brink of coming.

Heath quickened his strokes on Leah's clit, and she squeezed her eyes shut and threw her head back in ecstasy, calling out his name as she rode the wave of her orgasm. He followed her over, holding her tight as he filled the condom with his cum. He'd never known fucking could be so good. Never felt so connected to another person until Leah. He felt like the luckiest man in the world, but conflicted nonetheless.

They held each other while their breathing and pulses slowed. He'd be happy spending the rest of the evening with her in the closet rather than rejoining the festivities.

She kissed him lightly on the lips and slowly lifted herself off his softening erection. "We'd better get cleaned up and head back downstairs, don't you think?" she asked and stood up. He held on to her hips, keeping her steady.

Wishing they didn't have to go back downstairs, he sighed. He'd prefer more alone time with her. Regretfully, he stood up and gathered his clothes.

"I'll get cleaned up next door so we don't draw

any attention to ourselves and meet you downstairs." She still got embarrassed although she didn't need to. They were consenting adults, and it was no secret to their families or Cobras HQ they were together. For now, and he hoped for a long time to come.

Easy, buddy. One day at a time, remember?

She blushed and picked up her scattered clothes while he dressed. "Thanks, I'll see you downstairs." She gave him a quick peck on the cheek and dashed out of the closet, most likely to the en-suite bathroom to clean up.

After dressing and sneaking into the bedroom next door unseen, he discarded the condom and freshened up in the room's bathroom. He shook his head. Most of the eleven bedrooms had a full, luxurious en-suite bathroom. He didn't envy the cleaning staff Luke and Abbey must have hired to clean the estate. They'd need an army. Good thing his little brother was a billionaire.

He glanced in the vanity mirror before heading out to join everyone downstairs. He almost didn't recognize himself. Staring back at him was a man who looked satisfied, happy, but troubled. His eyes, looking greener than brown, still had some sparkle, and his complexion was flushed from his time with Leah in the other room.

He approached the bedroom door, which he'd left ajar in case Leah came looking for him, when he heard someone speaking in the hallway. He got as close to the door as he could without being noticed so he could listen.

"So, this thing with Leah and Heath, it's serious?" He heard who he thought was Tom Murphy say. Tom Murphy worked for the Chicago Cobras in IT.

Heath heard someone scoff. "It won't last. Someone like Leah will want a man who's all in one piece. I've asked her out a few times. From what I heard, she's been pining over Heath since before he joined the Marines. Then he got hurt and was discharged. Once she's had her fun we'll end up together. I'm better for her than Heath."

That came from corporate attorney for the Cobras Mel Johnson. *Motherfucking Mel.* He'd made a play for Abbey at Jake and Cassie's wedding, but Luke had shut him down immediately.

Heath backed away from the door. Mel's comments were like a punch to the gut. His worst fears realized and said aloud. Reality, which he'd tried to ignore up to this point, came crashing down around him. He knew Mel was right, not that he and Leah would end up together necessarily, but that she'd move on after a period of time and find a man who was "all in one piece" as he put it. She deserved someone better. Perfect and whole, physically and emotionally.

Being a Navy veteran though, he'd expected a little more from the man, but it didn't make what Mel said any less true. Heath had just been enjoying his time with Leah so much he ignored the inevitable truth. Their time together was limited. It always had been. He just hadn't wanted to admit it. Maybe he should thank Mel for reminding him of that fact.

Knowing what he'd have to do, Heath joined everyone on the first floor just as the women were heading to the sunroom. Leah turned to him, an angelic smile on her face, and waved. His heart ached for her and for what he knew he'd have to do, but he managed a tight smile and waved back, not wanting to let on how devastated he felt.

After the ladies were out of sight, his father came up to him with a concerned look on his face. He was glad his father came tonight, having not attended Jake and

Cassie's wedding and not planning on attending Luke and Abbey's either. His father was still mourning the sudden loss of his mother three years ago. He'd steered clear of weddings ever since.

"Everything all right, son?" his father asked.

Shit. Was he that obvious? He'd have to do a better job of acting like everything was fine instead of falling apart before he decided how he would deal with Leah.

"Sure, Dad, I'm fine." He tried to put on a brave, happy face for his father. He didn't want burden him with his personal shit.

His father narrowed his eyes, not seeming convinced, but nodded. "All right, if you say so."

That was good enough for Heath.

For the next hour he played along with the male guests in the estate's basement that was over twice the size of his townhome. Christ, Luke's place was huge. After winning five hundred bucks at poker, he feigned not feeling well and asked Jake to see Leah home safely. The look of disappointment and confusion on her face when he gave her quick peck on the cheek before leaving hurt him to his soul.

Tears ran down his face unchecked as he drove away from the only woman he'd ever loved. Why had he even started up with her in the first place when he *knew* they were doomed from the start? How would he survive without her? Did he even want to?

****

Leah stood at the left-hand side of the altar in Grace of God Lutheran Church, dutifully in her place between Abbey's sister and her own sister-in-law, Cassie, the matron of honor and Karla, Abbey's friend from graduate school who owned a popular coffee shop, Karla's Koffee Klatch in Lombard. Leah stood there with a smile plastered on her face, like a good bridesmaid should.

So far that day everyone had believed the happy façade she'd displayed, but she was anything but. She hadn't been feeling well and assumed she was coming down with a stomach bug since she'd vomited twice in the last week and she rarely did that.

But far worse than how she physically felt, was the emotional turmoil she'd experienced in the last week. And from the looks of things, that situation didn't appear to be changing anytime soon.

For over two months she'd been on cloud nine. It seemed like everything in her life had been going her way. She had a niece or nephew on the way, she loved her job and the condo complex she lived in, and she was in love with a wonderful man. A man who had told her repeatedly that he loved her and that she believed did.

Except since Abbey and Luke's housewarming and bachelorette/bachelor party exactly seven days ago, said man, who had seemed so sincere when he proclaimed his love, was gone. He had been replaced.

When Heath had left the housewarming party early and barely kissed her goodbye—on the cheek no less—she knew then something was wrong. She could see it on his handsome but troubled face.

And as she stood in a church filled with family, friends, professional athletes from various sports teams, and celebrities there to celebrate Abbey and Luke's wedding day, she felt like she was dying inside. Heath stood stoically just a few feet from her, so dashing in his charcoal grey tails, but he'd been miles away for the last seven days.

Even worse than the churning of her stomach and the dizziness she'd experienced earlier in the day was the fact she didn't know what was wrong. Before he'd seemingly flipped a switch after their sexy time in the walk-in closet in one of Abbey and Luke's many estate bedrooms, they had been fine. Better than fine.

Since then though, he'd spent no time alone with her, claiming he was busy helping Luke with "wedding shit". Even at the office he'd been cordial but somewhat cold, all business and too busy to have lunch with her. When she'd told him she loved him she'd only received a "me too" in response. And not a very enthusiastic "me too" at that.

Something was horribly wrong, but she didn't know what or what the hell to do about it. And to make matters worse, she had to act as if everything was fine when inside she was an emotional mess. How was she going to get through the entire day feeling like this? Why wouldn't Heath tell her what was going on?

Her mind refused to accept or believe this was most likely the beginning of the end for them. But in her heart and soul, she knew it probably was. It had to be. There was no other explanation for Heath's behavior. Why was he stringing her along by giving her the cold shoulder instead of calling it quits? Didn't she deserve better than that? *Damn straight, I sure as hell do.*

Abbey and Luke had opted for the traditional seating arrangement at the head table with the women seated on the groom's side and the men on the bride's. It was just as well. She couldn't stomach being close to Heath under the circumstances. Seated between Cassie and Karla during dinner she pushed her dinner around on her plate, barely able to tolerate a few bites. She did her best to engage them in conversation, to keep up appearances, but she felt dead inside.

"I met Grace Asher and Gino and Carlo Antonetti tonight," Karla commented happily.

Leah had also gotten the chance to meet Gino

Antonetti. Gino was a year younger than his oldest brother Carlo, the owner/manager of the three-restaurant chain, and could almost be mistaken for his twin. Leah and Grace had become close over the last two months, and she was proud to call the lovely southern belle her friend.

"Grace and I have become close. She's a great person. I noticed you and a certain dark-haired, bad boy, computer genius chatting a bit." Leah couldn't resist teasing Karla. She might be a successful small business owner offering the best damn coffee she'd ever tasted, but she'd learned Karla was shy with men. She didn't think anything was going on between her and Tom Murphy, Abbey's former coworker from Office Supply Galaxy and current IT—Information Technology employee for the Cobras though.

Karla blushed prettily like Leah knew she would and giggled. "He revamped the shop's computer system, and it's helped me get and stay even more organized. It's made a huge difference for me. He's a tech genius. And did Abbey tell you I'm in preliminary talks with Kyle Asher, Grace's brother, about Karla's Koffee Klatch joining Envy Entertainment's family of companies?" Karla's bright smile was infectious, and Leah smiled back.

"No. It's been pretty hectic these days, but that's amazing news. Congratulations," she replied. She was happy for Karla. She had something special going on with her coffee shop. Joining forces with Envy Entertainment was a smart move.

They all watched on as Abbey and Luke danced their first dance to "At Last" by Etta James. Fitting for the couple since they'd gotten back together after a bad breakup ten years before. Tears welled up when the bridal party was invited to the dance floor. She would have to face this new cold, distant Heath again.

Feeling zombie-like, she went to the dance floor alone to join Heath, who'd obviously not wanted to escort her there. They both stood there awkwardly for a moment before finally coming together, barely touching, but dancing along with everyone else.

She lost her patience at his indifference and silence just as the song ended. "What's going on with you this past week? What's wrong?" His cold shoulder routine and semi-silent treatment were bullshit, and she was done with it.

He sighed, and "We are Family" by Sister Sledge began playing. She felt for Luke and this song selection. Family meant everything to him. It did to her, too, which was why Heath's treatment over the last week hurt so much. They were family, and he was treating her like crap.

"Not now. Let's talk later," he said over the music and danced with their family close by on the dance floor.

Not wanting to cause a scene, she gritted her teeth and put on an Oscar-worthy performance as a happy bridal party member. Maybe dancing would help her shake off the anguish she was feeling over what was happening with Heath.

After nearly an hour of being put off, Leah seized her opportunity. She marched over to the bar with purpose where he'd just been handed a bottle of beer. Enough was enough. Time for her to woman up and for him to stop acting like a coward.

"We need to talk privately, Heath. Now." She was angry, unhappy, and ill all at the same time. *Keep it together, Leah.*

He locked eyes with her, and she felt her stomach drop to the floor. His cold, uncaring gaze made her shiver.

"Not now. I told you later."

That was it, she was done. "And I'm telling *you*, this *is* later. We can either talk here in front of everyone else, or in private in one of the empty banquet rooms," she said, raising her voice slightly. She noticed Grace of the corner of her eye stop her conversation and look over at her. She didn't want to make a scene at Abbey and Luke's wedding, but she couldn't take Heath's dismissal of her any longer. If he was letting her go, she preferred he did it now and got it over with.

He narrowed his green eyes, and she nearly stepped back. "Are you making demands, little girl?"

He was back to calling her "little girl"? She'd show him how little she was. She stood tall and pulled her shoulders back, her rage and sadness bubbling over. "I am."

"Fine, if you can't let it go." He grabbed her hand and dragged her out of the banquet room, past an extensive security detail, celebrities and professional athletes in the hallway, to a small empty banquet room near the restrooms. He slammed the door closed and turned to her with fire in his eyes.

"What the fuck has been going on with you? And don't tell me nothing because that's a lie." She tried to brace herself emotionally for what she believed was about to happen, but she felt nauseated. *Don't lose it. Not now.*

He sighed and briefly closed his eyes. When he opened them again, for a second she thought she saw sadness in the hazel green eyes she'd loved her entire life, but that sadness was quickly replaced with a neutral expression.

"I wanted to wait until after the wedding festivities were over to say something, but since you

insist on having this conversation *now*, I don't want to
see you anymore. As my girlfriend, I mean."

Her head spun, and her ears rang. The devastating
reality of Heath breaking up with her was too much to
bear. What a fool she'd been to think she could prepare
for being cast aside.

"Just like that? No conversation? You're done
with me, and that's that?" How could he stand there,
seemingly unaffected and let her go? Like she was some
random chick, not someone he'd known for twenty-five
years?

"No. Not just like that. When we started out we
agreed to take things slow and see how things went,
remember? And I've come to realize that I was right all
along. Us together isn't a good idea. I'm not what you
need. This is all just too much for me. You deserve better
than I can give you."

She didn't want to argue the point with him
again. What good would it do? She had enough pride to
not beg him to stay with her. But her emotions were all
over the place. At the moment she was furious. When
had he decided he was through with her?

"So at Abbey and Luke's housewarming last
week—what was that? One last fuck for the road? Way
to treat me like I'm some whore, rather than the woman
you *claimed* to love."

Heath approached her with a regretful expression
on his handsome face, but she stepped back. How could
she still find him attractive when he'd just torn her heart
to shreds?

"It's not like that, Leah. Come on. You've seen
what it's like with me. It's not easy. In time you'll see
I'm right about this," he whispered.

She was a grown woman, capable of determining
what was right and what she deserved. She didn't need

Heath or anyone else deciding what was best for her.

"You know what? Shut up. Just shut up and get out!" Like a fool, she'd hoped being upset would cause him to change his mind about ending things, but he seemed relieved and left without another word, clicking the door closed behind him.

Her tears fell, and she felt ready to collapse when just in the nick of time Grace's arms wrapped around her tightly. They stood together, in a comforting embrace in the empty banquet room. Grace swayed from side to side giving Leah a moment to grieve the loss of the love of her life.

"Can you take me home?" Leah asked between sobs.

Grace looked into her eyes as tears ran down her own face and nodded. "Of course. I'm here for you. Whatever you need."

• Chapter Nine

Two days later, Leah was brushing her teeth after vomiting yet again. This was the strangest stomach bug she'd ever had. Or this was what heartbreak did to a woman. Either way, she felt awful. Numb. Empty. Destroyed.

She was grateful she'd taken Thursday and Friday off after Abbey and Luke's wedding as she couldn't face anyone right now, let alone Heath. But what would happen on Monday? How could she go back to the office and act like everything was fine? Like he hadn't just used her to have his fun and then tossed her aside.

Her emotions had been all over the place since Abbey and Luke's housewarming and especially since Heath dumped her two days ago. Even as distraught as she felt now, she believed in her heart that Heath loved her. Or *had* loved her. The analyst in her wasn't able to reconcile the complete turnaround in his behavior or treatment of her though. In her mind, it didn't add up.

What the fuck did she know anyway? She'd been pining over a man her entire life. One she thought was decent. True. Honest. A hero. It seemed to her now as she looked back at her pathetic reflection in her vanity mirror, he wasn't all that different than all the other men out there. He'd used her love for him to his advantage, and when he'd had his fill, he discarded her. And like an idiot, she'd made it easy for him. Fawning all over him like he was God's gift to women. Some gift.

Her stomach roiled, and she turned to the toilet and took a deep breath while gripping the vanity countertop. Then she took another, slowly in and out. When she felt steady, she gradually made her way to the living room and threw herself on the couch.

She sure as hell wouldn't make that mistake ever again. If she bothered dating in the future, and based on how she felt at the moment, that was a *huge* if, she'd make sure the man in question *earned* her time and attention. She wouldn't make it easy. Never again. Although she may feel like death warmed over now, Heath had taught her a valuable lesson. No more free passes.

Flipping through the channels on her television, hoping to find something to lift her spirits, she startled when her cell phone rang. For a moment, hope bloomed that Heath had come to his senses and was calling to beg her to take him back. She immediately chastised herself for even considering it.

Seeing Grace's name on the phone display made her smile. That was one thing she could thank Heath for. Introducing her to her new close friend. She'd been so sweet at Abbey and Luke's wedding, taking her home after Heath had ripped the rug out from under her.

Grace hadn't just dumped her off at home and left her high and dry either. She'd stayed with Leah, wrapped her arms around her on the couch and held her while she cried her eyes out. She'd even cried herself. She couldn't have been any more supportive. Leah had felt like a heel cutting Grace's evening short. She answered the call, already feeling a little better, knowing Grace was thinking about her. "Hey."

"Hey there yourself, honey. Sorry it took me all day to call, but Golden Horns has been so busy since the grand opening. We need to hire more staff ASAP! How are you doing?" Grace's kindness resounded loud and clear through the phone. Just hearing her voice soothed Leah a little.

She leaned back on the couch and closed her eyes. "I'm doing all right. I threw up again. I can't seem to kick this stomach bug to the curb. I'm never sick, so it's really annoying. How are you?"

"Oh no! Again? Why haven't you gone to the doctor?" Grace asked, her concern unmistakable.

Leah frowned. She wasn't fond of doctors, hospitals, or needles and only went to the doctor when it was absolutely necessary. "Well … I thought I'd just give it a couple of days to work its way through my system."

"Have you been able to keep anything down? Have you been staying hydrated? You need to replenish the fluids you're losing," Grace advised her like a mother hen.

Leah smiled into the phone, but her stomach churned at the thought of food. "The thought of food makes me queasy, but I've been drinking plenty of water, Mom," she teased.

Grace sighed over the line. "Are you going to be home for a little while?"

She almost laughed. Where was she going to go? And with the way she was feeling, it was smart to stay near a bathroom. "I'm not going anywhere, but you don't have to come over. I've put you out enough, and I appreciate everything you've done. You've been amazing. Thank you." She didn't want to take advantage of Grace's kind nature. Leah was a big girl, and she could handle her shit.

Grace sighed dramatically. "Just don't go anywhere all right? I'll there in less than an hour. And if you can, drink more water and try and see if you can handle eating a few saltines if you have them."

The thought of saltines didn't send her stomach reeling, but she wasn't hungry. "I've got some but I'm not hungry."

"Fine," Grace huffed. "Just try and drink some

water until I get there."

The call ended before Leah could say anything else. Reluctantly, she went to the kitchen and grabbed a bottle of water from the fridge. She sipped while looking for saltines in her small pantry. She'd make an effort for Grace since she was being so nice to her.

Opening a sleeve of saltines and not feeling nauseated she slowly ate a cracker and waited. Smiling when she felt fine, she tried eating another and drank more water. About forty minutes after she'd hung up with Grace, Leah's buzzer rang.

"Hello," she said after pressing the intercom/buzzer button.

"Hey, honey, it's me, Grace."

Smiling and thankful to have company, she buzzed Grace in. She waited by the door, not taking any chances since Heath had scolded her about opening the door without using the peephole. She wouldn't hate him for that advice since it was for her own safety.

She checked before opening the door and was greeted by a concerned looking Grace holding a Walgreens bag. At least she was wearing jeans rather than a dress, which meant she was off Envy Entertainment's clock. The southern belle worked far too much as far as Leah was concerned.

"Have you been drinking water since we hung up? Did you try eating some crackers?" Grace asked immediately after Leah closed her condo door.

She rolled her eyes, trying to keep her attitude light. "Yes, I did. What's the big deal?" Why was Grace so concerned about her water consumption and eating habits? She knew Leah hadn't been feeling well.

Grace handed her the Walgreens bag. "This is the big deal. Take these."

"What's this?" After she opened the bag and saw

the contents, she tried to hand it back, but Grace wouldn't take it. "I don't need these."

"I hate to break it to you, but I think you're pregnant. I got three different tests that are supposed to be very accurate," Grace replied and crossed her arms in front of her.

Leah shook her head. She couldn't be pregnant. No way. "We've been careful. I can't be pregnant. It's a stomach bug or something. I'll stop being a baby about it and go to the doctor."

Grace didn't look convinced. "How careful were you? Are you on the pill and had Heath used condoms, too?"

"Well, no. But we always used condoms," she replied.

"Always?" Grace countered.

"Yes, every—" She thought back. They'd gone through multiple boxes of condoms over the last couple of months. They'd been careful every time. Then she remembered there had been the time up against her hotel room wall the night of Jake and Cassie's wedding. Their first time together. They'd both been so frantic to hook up they had forgotten to use one. *Shit.*

As tears threatened to fall, Grace hugged her. "Don't cry, Leah. Take the tests and know for sure, okay? I could be wrong, and it might just be a stomach bug or something, just like you said."

Five minutes later they both walked back into her master bathroom to check the results of the three tests. Tears spilled as Leah read three positives.

"Shit." She placed her hands on her stomach, stunned. Pregnant. With Heath's child. She'd dreamed of this day all of her life. She hadn't dreamed they wouldn't be together when it happened though. Now what?

Grace gently placed her hands on tops of hers.

"Any idea how far along you might be?"

She nodded. She knew exactly how far along she was. "Yeah, about two and half months. It happened the night Jake got married. I'm so stupid. When you called I thought it was Heath calling to say he'd made a mistake and that he wanted to be together after all."

"I'm so sorry. He's on shift as a DM tonight at Club Envidious as a favor to Kyle, so he doesn't have his phone with him," Grace whispered.

Wasn't that just great? Here she was pining over him like a schoolgirl, just found out he'd knocked her up, and what was *he* doing? He was "monitoring" people fucking. *Asshole.* He'd just moved on like she didn't even exist. Like she was no one.

Instead of feeling upset like she knew she would later, she was furious. Pissed off in fact. Well fuck him. She was Leah Tyler and would *not* be treated like she was nothing. Not by asshole, coward, "you deserve better" Heath Jackson. She tossed the pregnancy tests in the trash and set out to give him a piece of her mind. She was done being his doormat.

After a quick shower, thoughtfully selecting her sexiest jeans, which were a little tighter than usual now, and a purple V-neck sweater that showed ample cleavage thanks to her push-up bra, she waited for Grace to swipe the Club Envidious access card in front of the reader so they could enter. She was so ready to tell Heath off she was shaking.

"Are you sure about this?" Grace asked for the tenth time. "Maybe you should wait until you've calmed down and processed everything."

"Processed what?"

Where the hell had Rocco come from?

She turned to find a concerned Rocco in regular street clothes, a navy t-shirt, and black jeans. He lived on the third floor in one of the two-bedroom executive apartments. She supposed it wasn't surprising to see him, since as a tenant he still needed to enter through the front lobby to get to the apartment elevators on the non-club side of the building.

"It's nothing. Grace, please swipe the card. As my friend. As a woman," she pleaded.

"What does that mean?" Rocco asked.

Leah didn't answer. She had nothing against Rocco, but he was Heath's friend, his Marine brother, and she didn't want him involved. If he followed them inside like she expected him to, he'd know soon enough.

Grace nodded. "You're right." She swiped the keycard and opened the door that led to the lounge.

Leah spotted Doreen, who'd had Grace dye her hair back to its natural pretty brown color. She now wore a thong with her server's corset and the club collar. From what Grace had told her, Doreen had turned over a new leaf since she'd met her. She was working at Golden Horns part of the time as well.

But what if she really hadn't turned over a new leaf? What if this "new" Doreen was just some elaborate scheme to get back into Heath's good graces? What if Heath had dumped her because he wanted this *version* of Doreen instead of her? Heath could have her for all she cared. But she wouldn't allow her anywhere near her baby though. Of that, she was certain. She glared at Doreen and left the lounge to go find Heath in the dungeon. Rocco and Grace were hot on her heels.

The dungeon seemed busier than usual even for a Friday night. Weaving around club members and guests with determination she spotted Heath near Master Gideon, who was working his magic with colorful ropes. Heath wore the customary DM uniform of black leather pants and armband with a red DM stitched on it, and was bare chested. How could she be so angry but still find him attractive? She'd have to get over herself since they were through.

Once she was about a foot away from him she let loose, not caring who saw or heard her. She would have her say. "There you are, asshole. Picking up pointers to use on Doreen?"

"What are you talking about?" Doreen was right beside her. She must have followed her along with Grace and Rocco from the lounge.

"Give me a break, Doreen. No one's buying this *new you* crap. It doesn't matter anyway. You can have *Master* Heath."

Doreen's eyes widened, seemingly surprised. Leah almost felt sorry for her. Almost.

"Nothing's going on between me and Master Heath. I swear."

"Leah, what's going on? What are you doing here?" Heath approached her with what appeared to be longing in his eyes. She wasn't falling for it and backed up. She ignored the knot in her stomach when he looked hurt. Too bad. She was beyond hurt.

Leah waved a hand dismissively, at no one in particular. She wanted to say her piece and get on with her life. Things had changed for her in a big way, and she didn't have the time or the will to engage in club drama.

"I'm here to tell you that you were right. You're not what we need. You're not anywhere near good enough for us, and we deserve better. So much better than you." Their little group had drawn attention from nearby club members, but Leah was so upset she didn't let it bother her. Or stop her.

"Look, why don't we talk somewhere private?" Heath began and reached for her arm.

Leah backed away and bumped into Doreen. She

nudged her away with her elbow. "Stay the fuck away from me! I'm not going anywhere with you!" Doreen started crying, but she wouldn't let that stop her.

Before she could continue her tirade, Dr. Ted Hoffman maneuvered himself beside her, wearing black leather pants and black silk shirt with nearly all the buttons undone. "You don't have to settle for Jackson. Not when *I* can be your Dom," Ted informed everyone who was within earshot.

Damn. Not Ted. He'd tried a few times over the last two months to negotiate a scene between the three of them, even though she wore the club collar, and she and Heath had declined each time. He'd become a real pest. She touched her collarless neck and frowned while Ted smirked.

"Stay the hell away from her." This came from Heath.

As if he had any say in the matter. *The nerve.*

"Shut up! You don't get to decide who my Dom is." Not that she had any interest in Ted. She didn't.

"The sub can decide for herself, Jackson," Ted fired back.

What a jerk. No wonder he didn't have permanent submissive.

"Back the fuck off, Hoffman," Rocco growled and got up in Ted's face.

"Will you guys stop it? Ted, you're such a butt-munch. And you know what? No one likes a butt-munch, so stop being one. You might have better luck with women if you did."

Ted's mouth fell open, and she heard a few members snicker. The stunned expression on his face was priceless. His eyes narrowed, and he pursed his lips.

"You can't talk to me like that, little sub. Jackson's been too lenient with your training. I won't make that mistake with you."

Heath rushed Ted, catching him off guard and struck him in the jaw. Hard, nearly knocking Ted over. "You stay the fuck away from Leah. I mean it. She's off limits, asshole."

Rocco stepped in pulling Heath away from Ted as many club members stopped their play to watch *their* little show.

Leah wasn't impressed with Heath's possessive attitude considering how unceremoniously he'd dumped her two days before. "Screw that, Heath. You don't get to dictate who my Dom is, so cut that shit out." Dom was a strong word to describe Heath anyway. They only played in private, not inside the dungeon. Kyle had encouraged her and Heath to participate in the "traditional" lifestyle more, but they hadn't, preferring to keep things less intense, less formal.

Looking pleased, Ted smiled and nodded at her. "You see, Jackson? Do the decent thing and bow out."

Rocco held Heath back, preventing him from engaging Ted again.

"Get over yourself, Ted. I meant what I said. You're an amazing surgeon. No one is disputing that. But you're still a butt-munch and I'm not interested. And Heath, I quit. I've worked my ass off for the Cobras, so I expect—no, I *demand* an amazing reference letter from you *and* Roger." Roger was Leah's immediate supervisor. There was no way she could return to her job under these circumstances.

****

With a heavy heart, Heath watched his love elbow her way through the throng of club members who had gathered to watch the spectacle near the suspension apparatus, leave the dungeon. What a clusterfuck. It hurt his soul to see Leah so upset. *What did you expect?*

Rocco let him go, and he surveyed the aftermath of their confrontation. Ted was rubbing his jaw where he'd punched him. Heath felt a sense of satisfaction there. Ted was out of line making a play for Leah, and he damn well knew it. Leah was right—Ted *was* a buttmunch. Doreen and Grace were holding hands, distraught and crying. Many of the spectators were resuming their play, but Kyle, who must have been informed about what was going down, looked ready to blow a gasket. *Shit.*

"Doreen, get back to the lounge. You, you, you, and you. My office. Now," Kyle bellowed out pointing at Heath, Ted, Rocco, and Grace.

"What did I do?" Ted whined. "I'm the one who got hit."

"My office or your membership is revoked. Permanently." Kyle turned and began stalking away just as Ted's beeper went off. He stopped and turned back around to face them. "Ted, don't step foot back inside my dungeon until we talk."

Ted nodded, and he and Kyle left the play space.

The summoned stood, frozen in place for a moment before a sniffling Grace left the dungeon. Shortly thereafter Heath and Rocco followed suit. Once in Kyle's office the three of them took a seat in the leather chairs in front of his desk.

The only indication Kyle Asher's office resided in a BDSM club were the framed photographs of Master Gideon's models, male and female, bound in his colorful ropes that decorated the walls. Artistic, not pornographic was what they were. A true testament to the artist and model alike.

He'd taught Heath quite a bit over the last two months, but he doubted he'd ever become as skilled as the master. Seeing Leah bound in his ropes and then seeing the compression marks once she was unbound was a heady feeling. One Heath had missed for the last nine days. Nine days since he'd emotionally and then physically separated himself from Leah. Nine days of utter misery. And for what? She hadn't looked to be in any better condition than he was.

Kyle cleared his throat, bringing Heath out of his reverie. *Heads are going to roll.*

"So glad I have your attention now, Heath. Which one of you wants to explain what the fuck just happened in my club? Because the last time I checked, Dungeon slash play space policy number fifteen clearly states, among other things, please leave your intolerances at the door. If seeing a particular type of scene makes you uncomfortable, or if there is someone whom you have personal issues with (such as an ex or soon to be ex), it is imperative that you remove yourself from the situation *immediately*," Kyle said, reciting the policy verbatim.

"Kyle, I'm sorry for—" Heath began, but Kyle put a hand up, stopping him from continuing. Shit.

"Homophobic, heterophobic, biphobic, gender-phobic, leather-phobic, sex-phobic, or other biased remarks and attitudes, as well as *relationship* drama, will *not* be tolerated in *any* way, from *any* one. *No* exceptions. So again I ask, which one of you wants to explain what the *fuck* just happened in my club?" Kyle glared at them, waiting for someone to say something.

Before Heath could apologize, Rocco spoke up. "I saw Grace and Leah come into the lobby, and Leah looked really upset, begging Grace to let her inside. Inside the lounge Leah seemed to be angry with Doreen. She accused Heath and Doreen of being together in the dungeon just before you showed up. You saw what happened after that."

"Ted was way out of line with Leah," Grace said.

Heath couldn't agree more.

"Ted's been jealous of you and Leah, that's the problem," Rocco added.

"Butt-munch," Heath mumbled.

Kyle frowned, and Heath knew he'd fucked up. Chicago was the first leg of Envy Entertainment's expansion, and Kyle needed everything running smoothly. Relationship drama and fistfights in the dungeon were the opposite of smooth.

Heath wasn't even sure why he'd taken a DM shift tonight. Kyle had asked him as a last resort, and he hadn't wanted to disappoint his friend. He'd been miserable since the morning of Luke and Abbey's housewarming, his combat nightmare setting him off. Again. Although it was obvious Leah had been angry when she stormed into the dungeon, he'd been glad to see her. He'd missed her so much.

He'd been a fool to break things off like he had, but he truly believed he had done the right thing. Between his nightmares, PTSD related issues, and Mel's hurtful comments, he felt he had no choice. He only wanted the best for her, and he didn't think *he* was it. Not in his current state of mind.

When Ted had played up wanting to be Leah's Dom, he'd lost it. He couldn't stomach the thought of her with anyone else, let alone a butt-munch like Ted. Leah had him pegged all right. The man needed to get his shit together outside the hospital walls.

"I expected a lot more from you. What's going on?" Kyle produced a bottle of twenty-one-year-old Glenfiddich scotch from a desk drawer and two crystal tumblers. He looked to Grace and Rocco. "Baby girl? Rocco?"

After Grace and Rocco shook their heads, Kyle poured two fingers of the rich amber liquid into the tumblers. He slid a tumbler toward Heath, and he knocked his back in one gulp, while Kyle took a sip of his. He took a deep breath, looked at the glass and gestured two fingers. Kyle poured him another two fingers' worth, and Heath sat back in his chair with his glass in hand.

Heath took a small sip of the smooth, buttery amber libation. *What's going on?* That was a loaded question. He didn't want to get into it, but he knew he owed Kyle some sort of explanation. Since Leah and Grace had become close over the last two months he assumed she knew much of what had happened.

He explained, in broad strokes from his psychological issues since Afghanistan, to Leah witnessing and helping him after combat nightmares, to the hurtful comments Mel made at Luke and Abbey's. "So, I thought it would be best for her if I ended things and broke it off with her at Luke and Abbey's wedding. I hadn't seen her since, and then she showed up here and you know the rest."

"If you really believed not being with her was best for her then why did you care if Ted wanted to take your place?" Rocco asked with a smug look on his face.

Asshole.

"Because he's an idiot, that's why," Kyle answered.

Grace gasped. "Kyle!"

"No, baby girl. He is. I've got news for you, Heath. There are a lot of soldiers with *far* worse injuries than yours and with more severe cases of PTSD than yours who are happily partnered. Who weren't tossed aside after they were injured. When was the last time you spoke with Jasper?"

Jasper Reynolds had been Heath's counselor back in Texas after he'd been discharged. His office was in

Dallas, and he'd lost his left leg just above the knee during Desert Storm.

"Not for a long time. And Jasper's wife left him after he lost his leg, by the way." Heath was agitated. Kyle didn't understand. He never would. Only someone who had been knee deep in the shit could. Trying to explain it to Kyle was pointless.

"Because he treated his wife and son like shit after he got hurt. He left her no choice but to leave. And you know he's happily remarried now and has a decent relationship with his ex-wife *and* his son."

Heath sighed and rubbed his eyes. He didn't want to have this conversation. He didn't want their pity. Didn't want a debate. Wouldn't go 'round and 'round trying to make them understand.

"She deserves someone perfect. Like her. I'm so far from that now. You wouldn't understand, all right?"

"There's no such thing as perfect, man. Even without Afghanistan. You know that," Rocco countered.

"Says the man with a new chef's gig who just got engaged to the perfect woman and entrepreneur," Heath shot back.

"You think things with Hannah and me have been *perfect*? You know her mother, right? And the bullshit with Hannah's ex? And this thing with the grandmother? And my own shit I had to deal with? It's time you dealt with yours, too, brother. Have you looked into those non-medical PTSD treatments I emailed you? They'll make a difference. They have for me." Rocco glared at him.

No. Heath hadn't reviewed the information Rocco had emailed him. He hadn't seen much point. But if the treatments had helped Rocco, maybe they'd help him, too.

"Rocco's right. There is no such thing as perfect. What Rocco and Hannah have is perfect for *them*. What you and Leah have—had was perfect for *you*. But what did Leah mean when she said 'you're not what *we* need, you're not good enough for *us* and *we* deserve better'?" Kyle asked and then took a sip of his scotch.

Heath didn't know. Leah must have been so upset she wasn't thinking clearly. "I don't know. She was really upset."

"She was, but it sounded like she knew exactly what she was saying," Rocco countered.

Kyle's gaze zeroed in on Grace, who was examining her shoes, like she was purposely avoiding participating in the conversation. No, like she *knew* something. Of course she did. She and Leah were close now. She'd taken Leah home from Abbey and Luke's wedding after he'd broken things off with her.

"Baby girl? You wouldn't happen to know something you're not telling us, would you?" Kyle asked in an even tone, laced with suspicion.

When she didn't answer, Heath knew he was right. She *did* know something and was protecting Leah. While he respected the fact she wanted to be a loyal friend, he needed to understand what was going on.

"Please, Grace. If you know something, tell me," Heath begged. If he had any chance to making things right, he knew begging and groveling would be involved, and he'd have become a professional at both.

"It's really not for me to tell, but I think you're serious about trying to make things work with her." Grace sat up straight and looked him in the eye.

Heath nodded and hoped like hell she believed him.

"She used the words 'we' and 'us' because just before we came here tonight, she took three pregnancy tests and they were all positive. Leah was referring to her and the baby." Grace smiled warmly at him. "You're going to be a daddy."

Tears stung his eyes. He was stunned, and his ears rang. Leah was pregnant? With *his* child? *Holy shit.* He hadn't expected *that*. She must hate him so much considering how he'd treated her the last several days. His stomach sank to the floor. He was such an ass.

How was he going to make this up to her? If he could convince her to take him back, he'd make sure she knew every single day how much he loved and cherished her. He'd look into the PTSD treatments Rocco's brother researched. He'd get back in touch with Jasper. Whatever it took, he'd do it.

Grace's cell phone rang inside her purse as Heath swiped at the tears streaming down his face. She seemed confused as she looked at the display and held it up.

"That's Luke's number," he informed her. "Can you put it on speaker?" Luke and Abbey were in St. Lucia on their honeymoon, at the Providence St. Lucia resort Stryker Real Estate Holdings had recently acquired. He hoped nothing was wrong. What if it was Darren?

"Luke, what's wrong?" he called out.

"Heath? You're with Grace? It doesn't matter. What the fuck is wrong with you? My wife just got off the phone with a hysterical Leah. She didn't go into much detail, but it was pretty clear, *you're* the problem. You know what? I *knew* this would happen. I knew you'd fuck things up with her. Why Jake pushed a relationship between you two is beyond me. Just so you know, I'm with *her*. Whatever she needs, *I'm* there."

Heath's anger simmered. Luke could be a real asshole when he wanted to. "Stay out of it, Luke. Mind your own business. Get back to your wife, little brother. I've got this."

"I'm not staying out of anything. She's family,

and *I* take care of my family," Luke informed him with contempt in his voice.

"I'm warning you, Luke. For your own good, stay out of it. Or else," Heath replied back, his anger boiling over. He had enough problems without adding Luke to the mix. Luke was on his honeymoon for shit's sake. He needed to get back to Abbey.

Luke had the nerve to scoff on the other end of the line. "Or else what?"

Heath clenched his hands, shaking with rage. Was Luke serious? And what he could he possibly threaten Luke with? He was a billionaire. "Or I'll disown you," Heath blurted out before he could stop himself. *Fuck!*

Grace and Luke both gasped, and Grace started crying. Rocco shook his head with a disgusted look on his face. Kyle rolled his eyes.

"Oh yeah? Well ... fuck *you*! You're fired!"

Kyle threw his hands up. "That's enough! No one's disowning anyone and no one's getting fired. What is *wrong* with you two?"

"Is that Kyle? I know I called Grace's phone, but where the hell are you?" Luke demanded.

Kyle raised his hand, gesturing for Heath not to speak. Maybe he was right. Flaring tempers weren't going to help him with Leah. He needed a plan. An amazing plan. While Kyle calmly brought Luke up to speed, an idea formed that Heath hoped would convince her to take a chance on him for good.

"Thanks, Kyle. Heath, I'm sorry. I wasn't really going to fire you."

"I know. I wasn't going to disown you. I wouldn't even know how. But listen, I have a plan, and I'll need all of your help. It's a big ask." Heath had never done anything like this before. It had better work. If it didn't he was truly and royally fucked.

"I'm in," Luke was the first to say.

Heath was relieved when Kyle, Rocco, and Grace agreed to do their part to execute his plan. All that was left was for Leah to do her part when it was all over.

"Thank you, guys. I mean it," Heath said looking around the room at the best friends a man could ask for.

Rocco clapped him on the back smiling, seemingly pleased with his "get Leah back" plan. "We've got your back, brother, like you have ours."

Heath nodded and took a deep breath, feeling both relieved and terrified.

Here goes nothing—and everything.

• Chapter Ten

Heath checked his watch again for what felt like the hundredth time. Jake should be out of his meeting any minute. It was Friday morning, two weeks since the he'd last seen Leah at Club Envidious. She'd been so upset he still hurt. Being the source of her tears and pain ate at him.

He'd enlisted nearly everyone's help to make things right—Luke and Abbey, Kyle and Grace, Hannah and Rocco, and the Bellatoni family. He'd meant it when he'd told Luke he had a big ask. But if he pulled this plan off, he'd have it made.

Although he still wasn't sure he even deserved Leah or his unborn child after the way he'd treated her, he was back in counseling with Jasper Reynolds. They'd spoken several times over the last two weeks. He was dealing with his shit like Rocco had said he needed to do.

Tomorrow he would put his plan into action, but he needed to come clean with Jake before then. From a brief conversation he'd had with him over a week ago, Leah had told him they had broken up. And rather than tell Jake the truth, she'd just told him they had *both* decided they were better off as friends. Why she'd done it, he didn't know. Considering how angry and upset she was at Club Envidious, he wouldn't have blamed her for going straight to Jake with the awful truth. But because she was who she was, she'd spared him Jake's wrath.

It was ten after ten, and he was through waiting. Heading to Jake's office on the other side of their floor, he walked with determined strides. He wanted this conversation over with so he could concentrate on tomorrow's main event.

As he neared Jake's office he heard Mel Johnson

laughing from inside. Rage burned in his gut, and he clenched his hands. That motherfucker was going down.

Heath slammed Jake's office door closed once he was inside. He shoved Mel so hard against a bookcase some knickknacks toppled off the top shelf. "You stay the fuck away from Leah, you cock-sucking *squid*."

Stunned, it took Mel a second before he shoved Heath back. "I'll do whatever the fuck I want, fucking *jarhead*. Jealous you didn't score high enough on the AFQT's to join the Navy's elite?"

The AFQT, Armed Forces Qualification Test or military entrance exam score, determined what jobs a person qualified for in the military. Heath's score had been high enough to qualify for any position he wanted, including submarines. Mel had been an Aviation Electronics Technician in the Navy, so he presumably scored high as well.

"What are you guys doing?" Jake asked nervously, glancing at his closed door and then back at them.

Heath lunged at Mel again and clipped him in the jaw, and he fell over onto one of Jake's guest chairs. It had been years since he'd participated in hand to hand combat. The throbbing in his hand felt good, made him feel alive. "Sorry to disappoint you, asshole, but I scored a ninety-one. My great-grandfather served honorably in World War II and my grandfather in Korea. I *chose* the Marines to honor their time in the service. What the hell did *your* fucking family ever do?"

Mel quickly got up from his spot in the guest chair and barreled into him, punching him in the kidneys. His side burned. "I scored a ninety-three, motherfucker. My twin brother a ninety-four."

Jake was suddenly between them trying to push them apart. Heath wanted to push Jake aside so he could finish Mel off, but he wasn't about to risk hurting his best friend, his little brother, to do it.

"Okay, so you're both geniuses. Stop it or we're all going to get fired."

Mel rolled his eyes and scoffed. "Like Luke would fire the two of you. You're *family*. *I'm* the one who'll get canned, not you. Fuck! What's gotten into you, Heath?"

He wasn't so sure he and Jake couldn't get fired. The Cobras organization was Luke's legacy. They kept family and business separate.

"Not true," Jake said. "We had to sign the same employment contract everyone else does. Trust me, Luke would fire us if we violated policy. What just happened violates policy and you know that."

Heath didn't want to get fired. He liked his job. Needed his job with a baby on the way, regardless of if Leah took him back. A smile formed at the thought of her pregnant with his child. But Mel needed to be taken down a peg or two.

"Like I said, you stay the fuck away from Leah. Come near her again and I'll end you. I don't need perfect hearing to do it. I heard what you said at Luke's." Heath crossed his arms over his chest, daring the fucker to try something or deny what he'd heard in the hallway.

Jake looked between them, confusion on his face. Mel blushed slightly and sighed. He was busted.

"What happened at Luke's?" Jake asked.

Heath didn't want to get into specifics in reference to what was said about *him*. He was now getting help with his issues. "Mel over here has been harassing your sister."

Jake's eyes widened, and he lunged for Mel, grabbing him by his suit jacket collar. He shoved him up against the bookcase. *Dammit.*

"Did you hurt my little sister, you fucking asshole?"

Heath pulled Jake away from Mel, who to his credit, didn't appear to want to fight Jake. He was grateful. Jake wasn't a fighter, hadn't been trained like he and Mel had been.

"Calm down." Heath should have kept his mouth shut and let Mel leave without saying anything. But seeing him again was a painful reminder of everything that had happened after the conversation in the hallway. His life had gone to shit quick, and he blamed Mel, even though it were his own actions that led to his and Leah's current situation.

Mel righted his suit and tie. He put his hands up in surrender. "Enough, guys. I didn't know you overheard what I said in the hallway."

Jake turned to Heath, concern clear on his face. "What did he say? Be honest."

Before Heath could say anything, Mel spoke up. "I said a load of shit, that's what. I made comments about Leah biding her time with Heath until she moved on to someone else who wasn't hurt. Like me. I asked her out twice. *Respectfully*. Not in a harassing way. She turned me down both times. She was sweet about it, but she was clear she wasn't interested."

Heath ran a hand through his hair, his stomach in knots recalling the conversation. Unknowingly, Mel had spoken to his worst insecurities when it came to Leah. It had set off a chain of events he deeply regretted.

"All right. But don't think I won't ask her." Jake leaned up against his desk next to him.

Mel nodded and put his hands in his pockets. "Go ahead. I have nothing to hide." He gestured to Heath. "I meant no disrespect. You're lucky you made it out of Sangin with only the injuries you did. You lost members of your unit, didn't you?"

Heath could only nod. Though they were less frequent when he and Leah had initially gotten together, he couldn't shake the nightmares from Sangin. Getting injured, reliving the death of his brothers, both American and British, in battle, and sometimes not surviving the battle himself. But he was working on it though, with some of Rocco's brother's non-medical PTSD treatment suggestions and counseling. Turned out the guy had done his research, and Heath was hopeful.

"Your grandfathers would be proud of your service." Mel's sincerity rang true to Heath's hearing-assisted ears.

"Thank you, but I stand by what I said. Leah's *mine*. Stay away from her. That's *my* baby she's carrying, and don't ever forget that."

Heath had never seen Jake move so fast. Before he knew it, Jake punched him and he felt the sting of a split lip. Mel grabbed Jake by the shoulders and pulled him away, but Jake was pissed and struggled.

"No! I'm not afraid of Heath. Let him fight back. How dare you knock my sister up and then dump her like some asshole! She said you had *mutually* decided to break up." Jake was breathing heavily while he continued to struggle against Mel.

"I didn't know she was pregnant when I broke things off with her. Let me explain. That's why I came to see you. I wanted to come clean about everything that's going on and my plan to try and get her back."

Heath gestured to Mel to let Jake go, but he hesitated. Heath nodded, and Mel gradually let Jake go. Jake backed away and glared at him with a fierceness he'd never seen from him before. This was the first time in all the years they'd known each other that they'd come to blows.

It'll be all right once he calms down and I can explain.

"I'm going to try and make things right with her. Not because she's pregnant, but because I should never have broken things off in the first place," he tried to explain.

Jake paced his office, running his fingers through his hair. "You said you'd never hurt her. You got her pregnant," he whispered.

With Mel watching cautiously, Heath went Jake and stood directly in front him, stopping him from pacing. "We'd been careful after the first time that was unprotected. After your wedding I wanted her so badly, I got impatient and forgot a condom. I know you don't want details, and I won't give them, but I love her and—"

The quick knock at the door shouldn't have surprised them, but it did. "Jake? It's Pam. Is everything all right?"

He noticed Mel's expression soften as he finger-combed his hair and checked his tie. Did he have a thing for the new HR rep? Heath and Jake exchanged an amused look.

"Everything's fine. Just give me a second," Jake called out.

Mel looked at Heath and frowned. "Your lip's bleeding."

Heath wiped his lip with the back of his hand and winced. It stung like a bitch.

"I'm sorry, but—" Jake whispered.

"It's going to be all right, I promise," Heath said, hoping to assure him. He felt confident once he and Jake had a chance to talk, Jake would calm down and they could move forward.

The office was noticeably untidy, but they

couldn't keep Pam waiting forever. Mel had his hand of the office door waiting for the green light to open it. When Jake nodded, they all braced themselves.

"I hate to bother you, but I was told there was a problem," Pam said after walking into Jake's office. She glanced at Mel and blushed. She scanned the office and at him and frowned, seemingly unsure of what she had walked in on.

Mel smiled. So, there was something going on between Mel and Pam? *Interesting.* It appeared Mel hadn't been lying about just talking shit about him and Leah.

"No, no problem," Mel said right away. He looked to him and Jake pleadingly. "Right, guys?"

"But I was told it sounded like you were fighting."

Mel chuckled. "No, we got into a heated discussion about some of the team members and how the season's going," he said, obviously lying his ass off. "Why don't I explain everything to you in your office so Jake and Heath can get back to work?"

She glanced around the room again, with a suspicious expression on her face. Looking at Mel with what Heath thought was lust in her eyes, she nodded.

Mel smiled brightly and gestured to the door. After Pam walked out into the hallway he turned back. "You two going to be all right? Are we good now?"

"We're good," they both said in unison.

****

Leah picked up the manila envelope someone had partially slid under her door and let herself into her condo. She tossed her keys onto the kitchen table, and they landed with a loud clink. It was Saturday morning, just over two weeks since the scene at Club Envidious. She had felt decent, hadn't thrown up first thing for a change. Why she thought it would be a good idea to visit Jake and Cassie for breakfast at their place, she didn't know.

She knew why, because she'd been cooped up in her place for the last two weeks. Except for her first visit to the OB/GYN to confirm her pregnancy. Grace had come along. She hadn't wanted to go alone.

She'd held on to Grace's hand, and they'd both teared up when they saw her baby for the first time on the ultrasound screen and heard its racing heartbeat. The moment had been bittersweet. Her heart ached not having Heath there with her. He should have been. Was she going to face all future follow up visits alone? Or with someone other than the baby's father once she told everyone she was pregnant?

Her visit at Jake and Cassie's had been going fairly well in the beginning. She'd eaten some scrambled eggs and a few bites of a bagel without feeling nauseous. She'd considered that a win. Her morning sickness had subsided somewhat over the last week or so and for that she was grateful.

Once they started in with the baby talk, emotionally things had become difficult. She'd learned Cassie was having a boy, and Jake in typical male fashion, was elated. Miraculously she'd been able to hold back tears, when he showed off their newly completed nursery. All done up in blues, greens, and yellows with a baseball theme. She'd oohed and aahed when she thought she should, all the while wanting to bolt the hell out of there.

She dreaded the thought of putting a nursery together without the father's input or support. That's how she thought of Heath now—as "the father". She didn't expect he'd want much to do with her or her pregnancy. She wasn't sure if he'd want anything to do with his child either.

Turned out she didn't really know much about Heath at all. Even though it would tear her apart even more, she'd raise the baby on her own if Heath didn't want to be a part of their lives. She wouldn't force him into a relationship with her or their child if he didn't want it.

Leah wiped her tears away and slumped onto her living room couch. She tore open the envelope, assuming it was something from the condo's management office informing residents of some new policy or upcoming event.

What she found was a copy of her lease and a written note from Todd Myrick, her landlord Esther's only child and son. Her stomach churned as she read Todd's letter.

Ms. Tyler,

My mother, Esther Myrick, your landlord, passed away two weeks ago. This letter serves as notice that I am executing the vacate provision of your lease. You have thirty days from today to vacate the premises unless you wish to purchase the property for fair market value. Should you decide to vacate, you will be charged for the cost of making the unit fit for sale. I will be in touch with you in the next few days for your decision on the matter.

Regards,

Todd Myrick

Was Todd serious? Leah knew her lease terms, including the vacate provision. She knew from Esther, Todd's only motivation in life had become to give his gold-digging wife whatever she wanted. Selling Esther's condo would fetch him a pretty penny. Leah couldn't afford to buy it herself, even if she were working.

She had a healthy savings account, but with the baby coming and the time it would take to find a new job, assuming someone would hire a pregnant woman, she had to hold on to every penny. *Shit*. What was she going to do? With only thirty days to do it?

She placed a hand on her tummy and rubbed lightly as tears streamed down her face. "We're not off to a good start, are we?" she whispered. "Don't worry, I'll do whatever it takes to take good care of you—of us."

Leah sighed, feeling lost. Alone, kicked out of her place, no job and pregnant. Lost was only one of many emotions she was feeling at the moment. Leah's heart sank. She needed every penny, especially now.

She'd taken good care of the place. A coat of paint and a carpet cleaner was all she could see needed to be done to get the unit ready for showings. But with Todd's attitude and motivations, she couldn't count on him to be reasonable. And she couldn't afford a court battle right now.

After wiping her tear dampened cheeks, she dialed Grace. She needed help with such a tight deadline. She wasn't sure where to start and hoped Grace would lend a hand, even though she hated asking.

"Hey, hon, how are you feeling?"

Grace's upbeat demeanor caused her to sob into the phone. "Umm, my landlord passed away, and I have thirty days to move."

"Oh no! It's going to be all right. Don't worry. I'll come over, and we'll figure something out, okay?"

Leah sniffled, feeling awful yet relieved. "Are you sure? I really hate to impose."

"You're not imposing at all. I'm on my way," Grace assured her and ended the call.

She paced her place, checking it over for areas in need of repair. There really wasn't much to do other than a thorough cleaning, a coat of paint, and carpet cleaning. She prayed Todd saw reason and wouldn't try to gouge her on the costs.

After Grace arrived they both took a seat on the couch, and Leah watched on as Grace read over Todd's letter. She shook her head in disgust.

"What about your folks? Would they let you move back temporarily until you found another place?" Grace asked.

If Leah weren't pregnant she knew they would. But once they found out she was expecting, they'd insist she stay with them more long term. She wanted and needed to make it on her own, and she knew she could.

"They would, but I'd rather leave asking them as a last resort. Since I quit my job I might have to ask them, but I want to explore my other options first." She hoped Grace understood the mess she currently found herself in.

Grace frowned and nodded. She sat up and squared her shoulders. "All right. We'll save them as your last resort. I understand. I can research local moving companies. Why don't you call the leasing office and see if any other units are available? If you need a reference or co-signer, Kyle and I can help you out until you find a job."

Leah was touched by the offer but didn't want to take advantage. Who knew how long it would take to find another job?

"I can't ask you and Kyle to do that." She wouldn't do it. As generous as Grace's offer was, she still had her parents to fall back on. She wouldn't take advantage of their friendship or Grace and Kyle's kindness.

"You're not asking. We're offering, and it's only temporary. That's what friends do for each other, right?" The southern belle's smile was so warm and hopeful Leah gave in.

Hope bloomed. With their help initially, this could work. Leah had been a good tenant. There shouldn't be any reason management wouldn't allow her to rent a different unit. Feeling a little lighter emotionally, she called the management office. Grace was busy researching moving companies on her phone and making notes on the manila envelope Todd had left her.

She hung up feeling discouraged but not defeated. "They have three two-bedroom units that will be available in the next two and half months and a few one-bedrooms in the next three to four months," she informed Grace and frowned.

She watched Grace think for a moment. "We have a few two-bedroom apartments available in the club building if you're interested. And the DMs could help you move. They love showing off how strong they are. It would save you tons on moving costs. They'd probably take payment in the form of pizza and beer," Grace suggested with a smile.

Moving to the third floor in the Club Envidious building would solve her problems short term and save money, but she couldn't see herself staying long term. The club apartments weren't where she envisioned raising her child.

"Thanks, it's sweet of you to offer an apartment, too. I'll think about it, okay?" Leah hoped she hadn't hurt Grace's feelings.

Suddenly Leah remembered Luke and Abbey's beautiful luxury coach house. It was spacious, secure and private. Paradise Oaks Country Club, if Luke and Abbey let her live there, would be the perfect place for her and the baby.

Leah was almost giddy as she dialed Abbey. She hated bothering her during her honeymoon *again*, but time was of the essence. "Thanks, but I think I might have the perfect place if they're willing to rent it to me," she informed a seemingly confused Grace. She leaped to her feet, too nervous to sit still as she waited for Abbey to pick up.

"Hi, Leah."

"I'm so sorry to bother you on your honeymoon a second time, but I'm in a bind. I need to ask a big favor, and it can't wait." She paced the living room as Grace watched on, a hopeful expression on her face. Leah shrugged, hoping her idea would save her.

"It's ok, honest. How much lounging around can one person do, right? What's wrong? Of course we'll help, you know that," Abbey assured her.

Leah provided Abbey with the short version of her dilemma, leaving out her pregnancy for the moment. There would be time for that later, and she doubted it would affect their decision to let her stay at the coach house anyway.

"I'm so sorry this happened. Let me get Luke. I'll be right back."

Grace gestured to her, wondering what was going on. "Abbey went to get Luke. That's not a good sign, is it?" *Damn.* She had other options, but the coach house was the best long-term option of them all.

"They're married. It's something they both have to agree on, right? It'll be okay."

She nodded. Her heart raced, and she continued pacing as she waited for Luke.

"Leah, hi. Abbey told me what's going on. I'm sorry. I know you considered Esther a friend," Luke said.

She felt tears prick her eyes. Esther *had* been her friend. And because of Todd, she'd had her chance to say goodbye taken away.

"We're more than happy to let you stay in the

coach house. You'd be doing us a favor. At least it'll get some use rather than sitting empty," Luke assured her.

Leah did a little happy dance and gave Grace a thumbs-up, which she happily returned, smiling brightly. *Thank God. One problem solved at least.*

"And I want a lease. We can work out the details when you get back from your honeymoon. No arguments. I'm no freeloader, all right?" She recognized Luke and Abbey didn't need the rental income, but it was the principle of the matter. She would set a good example for her child and pay her way in life. Like she expected her child to do when they grew up.

Luke sighed on the line. "Fine, but not necessary. You're family. But if you insist, we'll hammer out the details when we get back," Luke conceded.

A few minutes later she was doing a happy dance with Grace in tow, both of them giggling. What a relief. It had been an emotionally brutal morning, and she was exhausted. She couldn't handle much more.

After a long hug, a few tears shared between them, Grace left. Leah felt optimistic about the future. She had an amazing group of friends and family and a wonderful place she could call home in the next couple of weeks. She smiled, for real, as she leaned against her door after Grace left. Things were looking up after the bombshell Todd brought to her door.

Leah'd been putting it off the last two weeks, but she couldn't any longer. She needed to look for another job. Seated at the desk she'd placed in the corner of the master bedroom, she brought up several jobsites on her laptop.

"Damn him," she muttered to herself. Scanning her email inbox, she didn't see anything from Heath or her former manager, Roger. She needed the reference letters she'd demanded two weeks ago.

Leah stared at her phone on the corner of the desk. She needed those letters. Bracing herself for what she hoped wouldn't be a stressful conversation, she dialed Heath. Her heart galloped in her chest and she shook slightly.

"Leah." The sound of Heath's low, sexy timbre made her body react immediately. She felt her sensitive nipples harden and her core slicken. *Traitorous body. He doesn't want you, remember?*

She inhaled deeply and centered herself despite her body's unwelcomed reaction to him. "It's been two weeks. I need my reference letters," she said hoping she sounded unaffected.

"I've got them. Why don't you come over so I can give them to you?"

Yes! No. "Email them. That's what I expected you to do." She wasn't sure being in the same room with him was a good idea. She was emotional, obviously still attracted to him, or to his voice at least, and she wasn't ready to tell him she was pregnant yet.

"Let's go over them together and make sure they're what you expected and I can make changes if I need to, and then I'll email them to you," he suggested. She'd rather not go, but he owed her kick-ass reference letters at the very least.

She sighed and shook her head, coming to terms with what she had to do to get the letters she desperately needed. "Fine. I'm on my way."

"Oh. Can you give me an hour? Please? I've got a few things I need to do first."

Jerk. He was pushing his luck. She quickly went from feeling aroused to annoyed. "Fine. I'll see you in an hour."

• Chapter Eleven

Heath hung up after a brief but tense conversation with Leah about her reference letters. A slow smile formed on his face. She was pissed, and even though it shouldn't, it made him hard. Hell, everything about her made him hard. He'd been such an idiot for letting her go. Jasper Reynolds, his counselor, and everyone else in the family had hammered that point home clearly. If this Hail Mary plan of his turned out to be an epic fail, he wasn't sure what he would do.

He checked his watch. His father was due any minute to help him with this part of the plan that Leah wouldn't even know about until years from now when their baby was much older. His heart fluttered in his chest for what seemed like the thousandth time since learning he was going to be a father.

He knew she was now just over three months along since they'd conceived the first time he'd taken her up against the wall of her hotel room on the night of Jake and Cassie's wedding. Aside from feeling like an asshole for not being careful like he should have been with Leah, his impending fatherhood brought him a sense of calm and purpose he hadn't felt since getting injured in Afghanistan.

He'd finished double checking everything the kitchen, from the plates, utensils, and napkins to the filled coolers with an assortment of beverages both alcoholic and not. Luke was on champagne patrol. Heath hoped there would be cause for celebration. Not for the first time he second guessed this part of the plan, which included their entire family. He was making a huge assumption or maybe he was just feeling confident in the outcome he wanted to achieve.

His doorbell rang, cutting his contemplation short. "That's Dad. For better or worse, it's time to get this show on the road," he muttered to himself. Considering his father hadn't participated in anything wedding related, other than attending Luke's housewarming and bachelor party, since his mother passed away, he was thankful he was willing to help him with this part of his plan.

His father's bright green eyes and a smile that actually reached them greeted him when he opened his front door. He breathed a sigh of relief. He didn't want to cause him undue distress. His father held up a digital camcorder and one-arm hugged him after he stepped inside.

"Son, she won't know if you look at what's downstairs. You know that, don't you?"

Heath led his father to the basement stairs. He pulled the black silk mask he'd used on Leah so many times out of his pocket. "*I'll* know. I don't want to take any chances."

About halfway down the stairs, he put the mask on and reached out to his father. "Dad, start filming." His father slowly led him down the remaining stairs until they were both in the basement. The previous owner had professionally finished the basement just before putting the townhouse on the market. And now, although he couldn't see it yet, it had been transformed into what he hoped Leah would consider amazing.

"Heath, I don't know much about this sort of thing, but what Hannah and Rocco did down here is incredible," his father whispered. The awe in his voice gave him hope his plan had a chance of working.

"That was your Grandpa Doug." Heath stilled. It was the first time referring to his father in that way. They hadn't discussed how he wanted his first grandchild to address him. His father squeezed his hand assuredly. Grandpa Doug it was.

"All right, it's me, your dad. Your Grandpa Doug is filming because I'm not supposed to see what the basement looks like until later after your mother sees it first." He let his father slowly guide him around the space as he filmed it for his future son or daughter. "Your mom, the most amazing and wonderful woman in the world, is just over three months along with you. We won't know your gender for a little while yet, so I'll explain what's going on from both perspectives for you real quick."

He was led into what he knew was now a temporary changing room. "I've known your mother since the day she was born, and I messed up. So badly. That's the truth. So badly that as your Grandpa is filming this, your mom and I aren't together—as a couple. And it's all my fault. Your Grandpa is filming part of my desperate plan—if you're a boy, a Hail Mary pass—to convince your mother to forgive me so we can be a couple again."

His father chuckled, and Heath smiled. His father led him back into the main living space of his basement, facemask still securely in place. Having lost much of his hearing due to his battle injuries, he wasn't fond of not having the sense of sight either, even if only temporarily. Leah had enjoyed using this mask during play, and he hoped he'd be securing it to her eyes again soon.

"If you're a girl, this is my grand gesture that will be preceded by a lot of begging and groveling first. But that's not something you'll need to worry about until you're at least thirty or forty."

More chuckling from his father caused Heath to chuckle himself. Not because he thought what he'd just said was funny but because anything with a dick that dared to come near his little girl, if that's what Leah was carrying, was in for a big surprise.

"I'm going to wrap this up now. The reason I'm in this position with your mother is because I got scared and ran away. It's that simple and yet that complicated. You're going to experience things in life that scare you. That change you. For me, that happened during my time in the Marines. I don't regret serving our country. It was my honor following in your great- and great-great-grandfather's footsteps. But even though the battles are over, the scars, guilt, and issues still remain. Instead of running away from your mother I should have worked through my issues, asked for help, which I finally did and moved forward, like I'm now trying to do and I hope you'll do, too."

Heath took a deep breath and gestured to his father to stop filming. Suddenly he was bear hugged by his father. He embraced him back as tears stung his eyes.

"I'm so proud of you, son. No matter what happens," his father whispered as they broke apart. His father took him by the hand back to the stairs, and they carefully made their way back to the first floor where he removed the mask. He wasn't doing *that* again any time soon.

Heath saw the emotion in his father's eyes. He understood he'd probably always feel his mother's loss, but Heath believed his father also needed help moving forward. "Dad, if everything goes the way I'm hoping they do today…"

His father patted his shoulder and nodded, a warm smile on his face. "I'm here with you from start to finish. You can't count on me."

"It's Jasper," Heath announced glancing at his ringing phone. He answered and set it on speaker. "Hey, Jasper, good timing. Dad and I just finished up downstairs."

"Great. So, how are you feeling? About your time downstairs? About executing your plan?"

Damn, just jump right in.

His father looked at him expectantly. He was a jumble of emotions, and he hated that. He certainly didn't enjoy feeling unsure. "I'm cautiously optimistic?"

"Are you asking me or telling me that's how you feel?"

Jasper really bugged the shit of out him sometimes. He supposed that was his job as his counselor, but it didn't make him feel any better right now.

With his father looking on he tried to put his feelings into words. "I'm thankful with everyone's help I could put this all together for her. But I've hurt her so badly. What if she doesn't want me back? Doesn't forgive me for being such an idiot? I'm fucking terrified. *That's* how I feel."

"You knew going into this that was a possibility. And if you're right and she doesn't want you back?" Jasper asked.

His biggest fear would be realized. He'd be wrecked, for real. If Leah didn't take him back, his heart would break into a million tiny pieces. Heath didn't know how he'd survive. But somehow, he'd have to make himself. For her and his child. This worst-case scenario would be a nightmare, but he'd have to make it work somehow. His father placed a gentle hand on his shoulder. He knew all too well what it felt like to lose someone you love.

"It would crush me. But like we've already talked about, I'd have to accept Leah's decision. And if we're not together as a couple, I'll do right by her and our baby. I'll work hard to be the best father I can be and support Leah in whatever way she needs."

What else could he do? If Leah didn't want him, he couldn't force her. Heath wanted her to be happy. He preferred it to be with him, but he had to consider the real possibility she could end up with another man somewhere down the line. He'd have to live with the regret of losing the best thing that ever happened to him.

"That's right. And I know you don't believe you ever will, but *if* you meet someone else you can love, you won't make the same mistakes you made with Leah, will you? I'm proof you can turn things around."

Jasper was right. Heath didn't believe he'd ever meet someone else he could love. Leah was it for him. He'd known it for a long time, but was too much of a coward to admit it and fight for her and himself like he should have, like she deserved him to.

He shrugged, knowing Jasper couldn't see him. "If that ever happens, which I seriously doubt, I won't make the same mistakes I made with Leah." His stomach knotted at the thought of having to see Leah happy with another man. A man who would live full-time with *his* child while he would be left with visitation days. How fucked up was *that*?

"But right now, we don't know what Leah will decide. I suggest you stick with cautiously optimistic for now. Right, Jasper?" said his father.

Jasper chuckled. "Absolutely right, Douglas. I think my work here is done. Keep me posted on what happens later. Eight o'clock sharp Monday morning?"

Heath was surprised by his father's nod. "I'll be there. It's my turn to call this time," his father reminded Jasper, who Heath thought was *his* therapist.

His father shrugged and handed him the video recorder. "You're not the only one who has issues he needs to work on. I'm following your lead and working some shit out."

He knew Jasper could help his father. He also knew his father would always love his mother. But at only sixty years old, there was no reason he shouldn't at least consider dating. And if he met the right woman, a relationship. He was proud of his father. Working with Jasper was a good first step in moving past the grief of losing his wife and moving on with his life.

Heath paced the first floor after his father left while he waited for Leah to arrive. The stakes were high. His entire future was on the line. He couldn't blow it. He needed to bring his A game. Hit one out of the park, to use a baseball analogy this time.

Heath heard the doorbell ring and rubbed the tiny velvet pouch in his pocket for good luck. This was it. His heart raced, and his hand shook as he opened the door.

Here goes nothing.

****

Leah didn't know what the hell she was doing. She should have insisted on Heath emailing her the reference letters, rather than making her come and pick them up personally.

Her hand shook as she rang Heath's doorbell. Her heart galloped so fast she thought it would burst out of her chest. She inhaled deeply. It would be fine. This visit should only take a few minutes. Maybe thirty at the most if Heath had to revise the letters.

She steeled herself as he opened the door. *I can do this.* It was all she could do not to throw herself at him. Not sure if it was pregnancy hormones or not, her body reacted immediately to seeing Heath in snug fitting black jeans that hugged his man parts just right. His short-sleeved, tight-fitting grey Marine t-shirt stretched tightly across his muscled chest and toned abs. His Semper Fi tattoo, among others, was on display, and the barbed wire tattoo peeked out sexily under his sleeve. Even the cut on his lip was sexy. It was so unfair. He had no right to be so gorgeous while she felt so broken, fat, and ugly.

She did her best to ignore her body's reaction. *It's just hormones. No, it's just Heath. It's always been Heath, damn him.*

Leah stood tall, hoping to display confidence and professionalism she didn't feel. Best to get this over with as quickly as possible. "I'm here, like you asked. Can I have my reference letters, please?"

There. She sounded calm and collected. At least she thought she did.

He sighed and motioned for her to enter. She stood in his foyer, uncomfortable. It felt unsettling and awkward after feeling right at home at his place the past couple of months.

"Let's go over everything in the living room," he said huskily, leading the way.

She followed obediently without saying a word. The view from behind was as arousing as the view from the front. His jeans molded to his tight ass and muscular thighs perfectly. She nearly moaned.

Wanting to speed things along, she sat in what used to be "her spot" at the end of his couch. She was relieved and disappointed he sat down on the coffee table directly in front of her, spread his legs slightly with a red file folder next to him. He leaned forward resting his arms on his thighs.

She resisted leaning toward him, but it wasn't easy. As hurt as she was, she still loved the man. She probably always would. And now because she was carrying his child, they'd forever be connected. Torture and pleasure all wrapped up in the man staring at her with such intensity in those hazel green eyes, she felt him down to her very soul.

Leah felt her resolve wavering. She wanted to tell Heath she loved him, missed him, and thought about him every minute of every day. She wanted to beg him to reconsider breaking up with her because even with everything he'd put her through, she believed with her whole heart, they belonged together. She always had. The child they'd created wasn't a mistake, although not planned, but a blessing.

"How are you feeling, babe?" he asked on a whisper.

Her heart raced as she assumed he must know she was pregnant. Disappointment filled her at the thought of Grace betraying her trust. She had believed they were close friends. That she could trust Grace with her secrets. It wasn't Grace's place to tell Heath, it was *hers*.

"Don't be upset with Grace. Kyle, Rocco, and I had her cornered. She didn't want to betray your trust. We didn't leave her much of a choice. She loves you, babe," he offered and got up off the table and kneeled down in front her, placing his hands on either side of her legs. She felt his body heat although he wasn't quite touching her.

Leah wiped a tear from her face. "Heath, I know…"

He placed a finger on her lips to stop her. That slight, gentle touch warmed her all over. She'd missed him terribly, wanted him so desperately, and needed him so much. If he rejected their child, she wasn't sure how she could go on. He may not want *her*, but their child was an innocent in their mess of a relationship.

"Let me tell you what *I* know. I was a fool to let you go. I let my issues, my insecurities, my PTSD keep me from the best thing that ever happened to me. I was a coward, breaking things off like I did. And so we're clear, my apology has nothing to do with the baby." Heath gently wiped the tears that streamed down her face.

Leah had wished for those words from the moment he had broken up with her at Luke and Abbey's wedding. But now after hearing them, she wasn't so sure she could trust them. And if she took a chance and he changed his mind again? She wouldn't survive the heartbreak a second time. Especially now that a baby was involved.

"How do I know you won't change your mind again? I'm not doing a back and forth with you. Baby or not. I don't deserve that." She loved him with all her heart, but she wasn't a pushover. She wouldn't be Heath's doormat. She had their baby to consider. She would set a good example and that included making sure she didn't let others walk all over her and treat her badly. That included Heath, especially Heath.

He sighed and closed his eyes briefly. When he took her hands in his she nearly melted on the spot, but managed to keep her composure. "No, you don't. You're right. I was so set on everything being perfect I just couldn't come to grips with the fact that *nothing* is perfect. Even if I hadn't gotten hurt in Afghanistan."

Leah nodded. She had understood that all along. It was Heath who had been so stubborn.

"It was Rocco who helped me to understand we have *our* kind of perfect. For us that means we know sign language. I have combat nightmares from Sangin that you can sometimes help chase away. That I suffer from PTSD and I haven't sought out treatment like I should have." He kissed her knuckles and gazed at her expectantly.

"Our perfect means we have three dentists in the family who nag us about flossing. And we have two sassy grandmas and billionaires thrown into the mix. And even though we like other sports, we are first and foremost a baseball family."

She laughed for what felt like the first time in a long time. She felt light and free but still unsure.

Heath squeezed her hands firmly and gazed into her eyes with such emotion she began crying again. "Our perfect is all that and more. Our perfect is now about the size of a lemon and has vocal cords, teeth, and fingerprints. An identity *we* created."

She nodded as the tears continued to fall. Their little baby did have an identity at this point. He must have read up on the stages of pregnancy. That knowledge warmed her heart. Maybe she *could* trust him. Maybe he finally understood there was a path forward for them. Their own kind of perfect. She liked that.

When he let go of her hands to reach into his pocket she nearly pulled him back. It had been too long since she'd last touched him, held him, and loved him.

"I know you're scared, but I'm asking you to have faith in me. In *us*," he said as he pulled out a small black velvet jewelry pouch from his front pants pocket. He retrieved a sparkling platinum set engagement ring with round center stone and two strands of accent stones on either side of the band. "I'm back in counseling and looking into effective non-medical PTSD treatments Rocco's brother Massimo researched. I want to be the best I can be for me, you, and the baby. And any other children we have in the future."

Her tears fell unchecked. He was putting forth his best effort. Taking their relationship and his issues seriously. She couldn't ask for anything more and would do her part as well.

He took her left hand in his, his hazel green eyes so intense as they bored into hers. She trembled as she waited for him to continue, knowing what was coming next. She'd dreamed of this moment over the years.

"I've loved you since the moment you came into existence. I'll continue loving you until my dying day. Will you marry me, babe?" Heath held the ring near her ring finger with an anxious expression on his handsome face. Leah noticed his hand shaking slightly while he waited for her answer. She knew she shouldn't, but she felt a small sense of satisfaction knowing he was nervous. He wasn't sure she'd say yes.

She palmed his warm cheek and felt a sense of feminine pride when he leaned into her touch. "I've loved you since the moment I realized you existed." That much was true. Even as a little girl she'd always known in her soul he belonged to her and she belonged to him. "I will marry you, and I'll love you until *my* dying day."

"What a relief," he sighed and slipped the ring on her finger. "Perfect fit, like us."

She'd only had a moment to admire her beautiful engagement ring before Heath sprang into action lifting her out of her seat. She wrapped her legs around his waist and held him tight as he walked straight to the first-floor master bedroom, which was currently being used as a guest bedroom.

Joy filled her heart when he gently placed her on the center of the bed like she was precious and fragile. She was unable to control the emotions that battled for space inside her, and tears fell. "I won't break, you know?"

A slow smile graced her warrior's face, and he nearly tore is t-shirt in his rush to get it off. Her eyes feasted on the beauty of the man before her. Muscles, scars, and sexy tattoos made up the man she couldn't live without. The man she'd loved her entire life. The man she would marry, the father of her child.

She'd missed him so much over the last couple of weeks that it felt more like months. Her body heated at the sight of him. Her already sensitive nipples ached, and her pussy pulsed needing Heath inside her.

She didn't waste any time and yanked her own shirt off, making quick work of undressing. It took a little effort getting out of her jeans as they were snugger now. A little pregnancy weight had made its presence known. She frowned, but couldn't take her eyes off Heath, who was now undressed and stroking his hard dick. Pre-cum glistened from the tip, and her mouth watered for a taste.

His hazel green eyes dilated, and his nostrils flared. The heat in his lustful gaze fueled the fire inside her. He crawled onto the bed and looked his fill. She tried not to feel self-conscious about the recent changes in her body, but she must have failed.

He shook his head, frowning. "Don't, babe. You're beautiful. Never doubt that."

He took possession of her mouth, and she moaned in relief. *Finally.* She wrapped her arms around his neck as their tongues danced and teased. This was what she'd been missing. The heat of his skin, the power of his body, the deep, passionate connection she'd never felt with anyone else. Her body trembled and ached, needing him so desperately. He ended their kiss much too soon, leaving them both gasping for air.

As he leaned back to look at her, her face heated. She'd gained a little weight with more to come as her pregnancy advanced.

With a tender smile on his face, he tenderly caressed her collarbone sending goosebumps along her flesh. He circled one pebbled nipple and then the other with a touch that was much too light for her liking. "Are they sore?"

"A little," she replied arching her back into his

hand. She needed his hands, tongue, and lips on her. Why was he torturing her by holding back? By taking things so slowly?

When he finally teased one tight bud with his hot, wet tongue she nearly came. It felt like a livewire straight to her clit. Moisture flooded her pussy as she endured Heath's agonizingly slow torment. After he attended to the other she was vibrating with need and panting.

"Heath, please," she pleaded on a whisper.

He just grinned a cocky little grin and continued on his slow, deliberate journey licking, kissing, and nibbling his way down her torso until he reached her lower abdomen. She felt the smile on his lips as he feathered kisses all over her belly. She reached down and ran her fingers through his thick locks as he greeted their unborn child, tears streaming down the sides of her face.

"Hey there, little one. I'm your daddy, and I love you and your mommy so, so much. I can't wait to meet you."

When she looked down she saw tears running down Heath's face and a look of such reverence she knew she'd never forget it. For all his doubts, demons, and hesitation she knew with certainty at that moment they'd always be together. He'd get the help he needed and would be a wonderful husband and father. They would have their "perfect for them" happily ever after. She was sure of it. She had faith in him and them.

He finally showed her mercy and devoured her pussy with his talented tongue, flicking her clit relentlessly until she was undulating her hips, chasing the orgasm that was building. She fisted the sheets, moaned and gasped for air. "Ss…so close."

Heath doubled his efforts, teasing and nibbling her clit until she saw stars behind her lids and succumbed to the waves of pleasure that crashed over her.

While she was still trying to catch her breath, Heath rubbed the tip of his hard cock along her slick slit and drove into her so hard she slid further up the bed, closer to the headboard. She'd missed how dominant in bed he was. He made her feel wanted, cherished, and sexy, like no one else ever had. No other had thrilled her the way he did.

Her pussy walls gripped his flesh, eliciting a moan from her warrior. A sense of feminine pride swelled inside her knowing she affected him as much as he did her.

"So fucking tight and mine. All mine," he growled and pistoned in and out of her so hard she felt another orgasm coiling in her belly, ready to snap.

"Say you're mine. You'll always be mine." He claimed her mouth, his tongue seeking hers. Her taste still lingered on him, fueling the flames of her desire even more. Heath gyrated his hips bumping up against her cervix as he continued to thrust in and out of her with all he had. The pleasurable pain was almost too much, but exactly what Leah needed.

She shattered and held him tightly, letting the rapture flow through her. Heath's thrusts became jerky as he followed her over. Her pussy convulsed around his shaft, fluttering over and over as he emptied himself deep inside her, no condom between them this time.

"Tell me you're mine, babe," he whispered in between gasps.

Waiting a moment until her breathing slowed, she cupped his warm cheek, smiling when he leaned into her touch. His hazel green eyes were filled with so much emotion it nearly brought her to tears.

"I've always been yours, you know that. And I always will be."

Of that she was certain. She had been her entire

life. If only Heath had surrendered to that fact sooner, they could have begun their lives together long before now.

She couldn't fault him entirely for being hesitant. There was their age difference, problematic especially when she was younger. Their families' close friendship as well his close friendship with her brother Jake. And lastly the tragedy in Afghanistan, which would affect him for the rest of his life, both physically and psychologically. It was a lot to come to terms with, and she was overjoyed he finally had.

Leah wasn't so naïve as to think the road ahead would be easy. Even under better circumstances, managing marriage, children, work, and family was challenging. She had faith they could make it work, as long as they were honest with each other and sought help when it was needed. The fact that Heath had resumed counseling and was willing to try other methods to cope with PTSD meant he took their relationship and his psychological health seriously. She couldn't ask any more of him than that.

Leah felt him softening inside her, and they both sighed. She was anxious to have him again, bareback. Nothing compared to the feel of him skin to skin.

He frowned and pulled out of her, resting on his elbows. "Thank you for having faith in me and giving me a chance. I promise I won't let you or the baby down." He kissed her lightly on the forehead, each cheek and ferociously claimed her mouth, causing her body to go up in flames again. She felt his cock harden again and instinctively spread her legs, eager to feel him inside her once more.

He cursed under his breath when his cellphone chimed with an incoming text from the other room. She giggled, not able to stop herself. "Ignore it." She reached between them to his now rock-hard cock and positioned it at her opening.

To her disappointment, he pulled away and got out of bed. "I can't, babe, but I'll be right back." Before she knew it, she was looking at his sexy, muscled ass as he strode out the bedroom door. She heard two more text chimes and then his phone rang. She sat up and tried to listen in on his side of the muffled conversation. *Shit.* He was speaking too softly for her to understand what he was saying.

****

Heath hung up after a quick conversation with Luke. Plans were in motion and with a smile on his face he padded back to the bedroom. His heart sank when he saw Leah sitting on the edge of the bed with a frown on her face. She had to know there was nothing to worry about. They were together now and would be forever.

She worried her bottom lip and looked up at him apprehensively. He smiled back, hoping to assure her everything was fine. He was relieved when he reached out to her and she stood up and took a hold of his hands. His heart swelled with love for the woman he'd known since the day she arrived into the world.

He kissed the knuckles of her hands and inhaled. The scent of her musk and sex still lingered in the air. He felt himself get hard, but they didn't have time to waste. They had thirty minutes to be exact before all hell broke loose—in what he hoped she considered a good way.

"Is everything all right?" she asked hesitantly, concern etched on her lovely face.

"Yes, it's perfect, well almost. We've got half an hour before…" He led her to the en-suite bathroom and turned on the shower. While the water heated he clipped Leah's hair on top of her head.

"What happens in half an hour?" She dutifully let

him guide her under the warm shower spray. He was humbled by her trust, still not sure if he deserved it, but he'd work on that.

"The rest of my Hail Mary pass plan," he said simply and soaped up his hands. He lathered up her now fuller breasts and had Leah moaning while he tweaked her pebbled nipples. His shaft was painfully hard again, eager for more time inside her tight heat. They didn't have a lot of time, so he couldn't linger like he wanted to.

He soaped up her torso, enjoying the feel of her wet, slippery skin. He paused over her tummy, which to him, didn't look swollen with pregnancy yet.

"I'm gaining weight," Leah complained.

Heath chuckled and shook his head. "Babe, I can't even tell you're pregnant yet. It just looks like you've gained a few pounds. I think you look sexy as fuck." He slid his soapy hands between her legs and teased her wet slit and swollen clit until she writhed against his fingers and had to grip his shoulders for support.

"Heath, please," she pleaded, moaning loudly, trying to fuck his fingers. He slid two digits inside her burning hot pussy, and she clenched around him.

"You want my hard dick, babe? You want me to fuck you again?" Heath knew the answer but wanted to hear her say it. He also knew at this point in her pregnancy her morning sickness was easing and she'd be hornier. Heath was more than happy to oblige his fiancée, soon-to-be wife, and mother of his child. He turned her around so her luscious ass faced him. She braced herself against the shower wall and enthusiastically spread her legs for him. His woman was ready for him. It was a heady feeling he'd never tire of.

"Yes, I need you to fuck me again. We have to

hurry, right?" She wiggled her ass at him, like the temptress she was.

He spanked one rounded globe, and she squealed. He chuckled and positioned himself at her entrance. "You're right, we do. But later tonight, I'll take my time and fuck you again and again."

He plunged into her hot, wet pussy with one single thrust until he buried himself inside her balls deep. They both groaned, and he fucked her hard and fast. Her pussy clamped around his thickness, and he nearly came right then. He reached around and stroked her nub over and over until she screamed out her release. He knew he'd never tire of hearing her passionate cries and looked forward to many years of satisfying his woman.

His spine tingled, and his balls drew up as he followed her over, emptying himself inside of her until he had nothing left to give. He came so hard his ass muscles ached. He held her tightly from behind as they slowly came back down to earth. Although he was looking forward to what happened next, he wanted to linger right where they were. Heath sighed, disappointed, knowing they had to finish up their time in the shower.

They made quick work of washing up, and Heath enjoyed toweling Leah's ripe body dry until she was ready to get dressed. He couldn't take his eyes off her as she put her clothes back on, one garment at a time.

"I've been training a little with Master Gideon these last two weeks. He's been helping me with rope knots and patterns that will be beautiful as your pregnancy progresses. He'd like to do a pictorial with you and a few other pregnant Club Envidious members if you're agreeable to the idea." She'd been working on her shyness in front of others at the club and being pregnant he recognized she might feel even more self-conscious. She didn't need to be though. Leah would be absolutely gorgeous as her pregnancy progressed.

She let her hair out of the clips, and it fell in soft, sensual waves around her shoulders. Heath was one lucky fucker to have her. He would make sure she'd never regret forgiving him.

He watched closely as she considered his request. It was a big ask for her, and he wouldn't be upset if she refused, which he expected her to do "Can he take the pictures so you can't see my face?"

He'd anticipated this question while he trained with Gideon, and they discussed the project. "Absolutely, if that's what you want. He's got no problem with it. We talked about his vision for this pictorial, it's going to be amazing—a real work of art. I'm good with whatever you decide."

Her smile lit up the room, but she shrugged. "I'll think about it, but I don't mind you trying out what you learned in private. Is that all right?"

He laughed and held her soft, warm curves in his arms. Yeah, he was one lucky fucker all right. "It's more than all right."

The doorbell rang, and he gazed into her loving eyes. "It's time for what's next."

A confused expression appeared her lovely face. "Next?"

He led her by the hand to the front door. "It's all a part of my plan to get you back. Just relax and have fun. Can you do that for me?"

She giggled and nodded. "After how crummy these past couple of weeks have been, I'm ready for as much fun as I can get."

• Chapter Twelve

Leah snuck another glance at her engagement ring as their family and friends around her finished up their meals. It turned out what was "next" in Heath's plan to win her back was an engagement party, complete with delicious food from Cucina Antonetti's and Golden Horns along with expensive champagne courtesy of Luke. She'd had a splash mixed with a full glass sparkling cranberry juice when her father and Darren offered toasts to her and Heath.

Although Luke and Abbey seemed genuinely excited to be there, she couldn't help but feel guilty for being the reason they cut their honeymoon short. She'd figured out a way to make it up to them.

She stood hand in hand with Heath watching their brood from a corner in Heath's living room, feeling a sense of joy and rightness liked she'd never experienced before. This was how things were supposed to be. Meant to be. She knew things weren't "perfect" and there would be challenges ahead, but she felt like the luckiest woman in the world. She'd take her and Heath's kind of perfect any day.

Her brother Jake approached them with a smirk on his face. He cocked his head toward Heath. "How's the lip, big brother? I don't think I marred that pretty face of yours too badly."

Leah's mouth fell open. She'd meant to ask Heath about his lip but had been distracted since the moment she'd walked through his front door. Never in a million years would she have guessed her brother would strike out at Heath. She'd never known them to have anything more than insignificant disagreements over the years.

Heath smirked back at her brother and shrugged.

"I'll survive."

She didn't notice any marks on Jake's face. Proof that whatever had happened, Heath hadn't struck Jake back. Considering Heath's military training, she was surprised her brother hit him in the first place. Jake didn't stand a chance against Heath if he fought back.

Her heart sank as she suspected their fight may have had something to do with her. "Why did you feel the need to hit my fiancé?"

Jake turned and gazed lovingly at Cassie. She was enjoying a hearty serving of dessert with a smile on her face, her five-month plus baby bump on full display. Leah's hand went to her own belly, still essentially flat but not for too much longer.

He turned back to her with a serious expression on his face. "Just a misunderstanding. Nothing to worry about."

Leah was having none of that. She poked her brother in the shoulder, and he took a step back. "Heath and I are together, so you better get used to it. No more fights, especially because of me. Got it?"

Heath squeezed her hand, probably hoping to calm her down. It wouldn't work. She couldn't have two of the most important men in her life at odds.

"And you'll always be my little sister. As long as Heath does right by you, there won't be any problems between us," Jake said through gritted teeth.

Heath lifted her hand to his lips and kissed it gently. Heat rushed through her, and her pulse sped up. He was playing dirty, and he knew it. He raised a brow and flashed her a cocky grin. "Don't be too hard on your brother. He thought I dumped you because you were pregnant. I would have done the same thing if I thought Greg had dumped Sylvia if she was pregnant. I would have done much worse than split his lip."

Jake nodded in agreement. "See? That's what big brothers are *supposed* to do. Defend their sisters. And speaking of defending sisters, did Mel Johnson ever harass you at the office?"

Heath tensed beside her. They were concerned about Mel? *What the hell for?* "No, he never harassed me. What's going on? Did you hit Mel, too?" Leah looked between Heath and Jake, trying to discern if something else had happened she needed to be made aware of.

Heath relaxed somewhat and glanced at Jake conspiratorially. "We just wanted to make sure. He said he'd asked you out a couple of times."

"We wanted to make sure he wasn't aggressive with you," Jake said.

Leah rolled her eyes. "Of course he wasn't. He asked me to dinner twice. He was very nice, not aggressive or creepy. I refused both times, but I wasn't mean about it. We're work friends. You didn't hit him, too, did you?"

Jake and Heath both chuckled. "There were a few misunderstandings yesterday. I promise, everything's fine." Jake kissed her cheek and shook Heath's hand. "I'm getting back to Cassie. Maybe see if I can get a bite or two of dessert. Congratulations again."

Leah noticed Kyle and Grace speaking to her parents. She couldn't imagine what they were taking about. She watched as Kyle excused himself and walk over to them. He gave her a quick peck on the cheek and man hugged Heath.

With a smile that showed off his dimples he didn't look much like a Dom or kinky club owner. "So, have you given any thought to a collaring ceremony, registering Leah as your submissive at the club and executing an official Club Envidious contract?"

Heath frowned. Kyle hadn't been subtle about his desire for the two of them to be more active at the club and the lifestyle. But as far as she was concerned, she liked things the way they were, private and less formal. She believed Heath felt the same way. She did have some diamonds that needed setting, though.

"I don't think we need anything as formal as a ceremony, registry, or contract. Luke offered to set the diamonds from our bridesmaid's hair combs. Maybe we could make a necklace or bracelet I could wear every day, as a simple symbol of the way *we're* choosing to participate. People do that, right, Kyle?" She didn't want to hurt Kyle's feelings by not embracing the full lifestyle like he'd been hoping she and Heath would do.

Kyle winked at Heath and snickered. "You've got one smart woman here, Heath. Yes, people do that. They select something that seems ordinary so they can wear it when they're not at the club. A necklace, bracelet, anklet—something with significance to both partners."

Heath's lustful green gaze bored into her with such intensity she could have asked everyone to leave so she could get him alone again. "I'm good with that. I'm with Leah. For now, we don't need anything formal like a ceremony and the rest. Not the way we're participating at the moment. If that changes somewhere down the line, we can do it up right at the club." He claimed her lips and kissed her so deeply she got lightheaded. She was about to sneak him away to the bathroom for some quick private time but heard someone clear their throat.

She opened her eyes to find Kyle gone and her Grandma Beverly and Grandma Ruth had joined them, both with sassy smiles on their faces and waggling their eyebrows. Her face heated, and she giggled.

Heath hugged and kissed them both on the cheek and wrapped his arm around her possessively. She leaned into him, not wanting to be anywhere else but beside him.

Grandma Bev was the first to speak up. "I'm glad you finally got your head out of your ass and did right by my little girl. I'd hate to have to kick some Marine ass, but I'd do it." Leah *thought* her grandmother was teasing, but couldn't be sure.

"It's a shame though, Bev," Grandma Ruth said, "He's got a mighty fine ass on him, you know?"

Bev let out a little growl, and Leah chuckled as Heath blushed. She couldn't agree more. He had a *great* ass, and it was all hers.

Grandma Bev eyed Ruth skeptically. "What the hell was that?"

Ruth growled again. "I'm a cougar, growling at fresh young meat."

She'd never seen Heath so embarrassed before, and it was endearing. Her big, bad Marine's face and ears were a deep shade of pink. God, she loved these two ladies.

Grandma Beverly rolled her eyes and shook her head at Ruth. "You're no cougar. Cougars are in their forties. We're long past that. We're cheetahs now."

Grandma Ruth frowned, seemingly confused. "Cheetahs? What do you mean?"

Beverly shook her head. "Congratulations, kids. We couldn't be happier for you both. Let me go explain the feline scale to this one before she embarrasses us any further." Beverly hooked arms with Ruth and led her away as she tried to explain the age groups that belonged to what feline.

She and Heath both laughed until tears sprang to their eyes. "Feline scale," Heath asked as he wiped away his eyes.

She shrugged, unsure herself. "You do have a

really nice ass, by the way. Maybe we need to check the interwebs for the feline scale," she suggested.

Heath scoffed and shook his head with a smile on his delectable lips. "Later," he said. "But first we need to talk about what's next," he nearly shouted and glanced around.

"What are you looking for?" Leah glanced around their party, unsure of what Heath was looking for. *Next?* There was something more than their wonderful engagement party?

"We need to talk about what's next," he bellowed out louder.

Luke appeared suddenly, wearing the black top hat she and Heath had been using during their sexy exploits. What was it about that hat?

"Sorry, man," Luke said, appearing embarrassed. "What's next is Heath doesn't want to waste time on a long engagement. A sentiment I can understand."

Everyone within earshot chuckled. They hadn't discussed a wedding date yet. She would show soon and wasn't fond of the idea of walking down the aisle as big as a whale. Maybe they should wait until after the baby was born?

"So, Leah, what do think about your wedding being the first destination wedding at Providence St. Lucia under Stryker ownership next Saturday?"

Leah and many of their guests gasped. She loved the idea. She'd never been to St. Lucia, let alone a luxury resort like it had been described to her.

Her head swam with everything that needed to be arranged. A week was a crazy short amount of time. She assumed the resort had staff in place to handle the food, flowers, and all the other details. But still.

Her main concern was a dress. What would she find that she liked, other than the Bellatoni couture gown she'd seen online while they waited for Abbey's custom-made gown to be made? She'd found the dress of her dreams, although she knew she'd never own it. It cost nearly as much as her car. Maybe she could find a floor sample that would do at a local bridal salon?

Luke handed her a business card. "The wedding coordinator is waiting for your call. She'll go over everything with you and Heath. Help you with all the choices. The resort's website has an extensive events page so you can see everything Providence has to offer."

Heath held her tight, and most of their guests had made their way closer so they wouldn't miss any of the conversation. "What do you think, babe? Will you marry me in a week? In paradise?"

She was overwhelmed. Heath's efforts to make her happy meant the world to her. More than some designer dress. She'd marry him in cutoffs and a t-shirt. As long as they were together. She swiped at the tears that suddenly fell and nodded. Everyone applauded.

Luke motioned for everyone to quiet down. "And we're bringing the family down, too. You're all welcome to stay as long as you want. We've got the permanent family villas set up and waiting for all of you." That got everyone's attention.

"The cheetahs will be on the prowl in St. Lucia! Look out," Grandma Ruth exclaimed.

"And don't worry, we won't infringe on your alone time. Your villa is a short distance from the main resort and has everything you need. The room service menu is outstanding. If you want to venture out and spend time with us, that's great. If you don't, there's plenty for us to do. Start packing everyone because we leave Friday morning." Luke winked at Abbey from across the room, and she shook her head with a grin on her face. "You might not see much of Abbey and me either for that matter," he said to the room and waggled his eyebrows.

"What do you think, babe? I know it's not traditional, but I like it," Heath said.

Leah couldn't agree more. It was their kind of perfect, and she couldn't wait. "Thank you so much, Luke. It all sounds amazing." She hugged him tight and returned to Heath's side, their hands interlocked.

Rocco and Hannah made their way toward them hand in hand as Luke stepped aside. Off to the side, near the basement stairs she noticed a man with what looked like a professional television video camera on his shoulder. A pretty, olive-skinned woman with lovely dark brown hair who she didn't know stood next to him smiling. She had a yellow tape measure around her neck and something on her wrist she couldn't decipher. *What the hell?*

"This is next," Heath whispered in her ear.

Rocco cleared his throat, and everyone quieted down. "The wedding is only a week away, and every bride deserves the dress of her dreams. A little piece of bliss she'll wear." He looked lovingly into Hannah's eyes and kissed her tenderly. The two of them radiated such love and emotion between them it almost brought Leah to tears.

"That being said, ladies, if you'll please make your way to the basement and let's help Leah select her Bellatoni designer wedding gown," Hannah bellowed out, pointing toward the basement door.

Leah's tears fell, and Heath hugged her tight. She was so stunned, she was shaking.

"It took a little while to arrange this part or we would already be in St. Lucia by now." He wiped her tears and cupped her face with his warm, powerful hands. His warmth seeped through her, and she swooned. His loving smile soothed her soul.

"You didn't need to do all of this." She was overwhelmed, blown away by this plan he and their family had put together for her.

He shook his head and brushed his lips against hers much too quickly. "Yes, I did. I want you to understand how sorry I am for putting you through hell and how much you mean to me." Luke handed them each their cell phones. Heath made a call, and her phone rang.

She picked up but didn't speak. She waited for Heath's instructions since it appeared he had every moment of this day planned.

"Put it on speaker and bring it downstairs with you. I want to hear everything, even though I can't see what's happening. That's tradition, right? I'm not supposed to see your dress until our wedding day." He looked at her excitedly, his eyes gleaming. He was enjoying this as much she was. He did put her through hell, but he was making up for it in a big way. Her heart swelled with such love she thought it would burst.

"That's right," her mother said and hooked an arm through hers. "Let's help my little girl pick out her wedding dress!"

All the women followed the camera man and the mystery woman down to Heath's basement. She heard squealing before she and her mother had descended the entire staircase. "Come on, honey, you've got to get down there," her mother urged.

Leah stood in awe, her mouth open in the main basement space. She blinked a few times, thinking she was dreaming. "Babe," Heath called out from her cell phone speaker. "What do you think?"

Hannah took her by the hand and led her further into the basement's main living space toward the center. What did she think? She thought she'd just stepped onto a scaled down set from *Say Yes to the Dress*. All the ladies sat in white overstuffed couches and chairs with Yes/No paddles and were sipping on champagne and juice, chatting excitedly amongst themselves. Her mother was now among them.

In one end of the room, full length mirrors lined the walls, surrounding a round short mirrored pedestal where Leah would model dresses for everyone's opinion. In the other were three racks with what looked like twenty stunning Bellatoni designer gowns. Next to the dresses were shelves and racks displaying bridal shoes, accessories, and veils. It was all beyond gorgeous and was all for her. She felt like a princess in her own personal fairytale.

"I think this is amazing. Is Randy Fenoli or Monte Durham from *Say Yes to the Dress* here? Is that why the cameraman is here? Is this a special episode?" she asked. Randy Fenoli appeared on the New York show that took place at Klienfeld Bridal, and Monte Durham appeared on the Atlanta show that took place at Bridals by Lori.

"Not exactly, Leah," Rocco answered. "Go ahead, Hannah."

Hannah motioned for the cameraman to begin filming. "We'll need everyone to sign waivers before they leave," Hannah said to the room. "This will be the first episode of a new Chicago-based show that takes place at what used to be Blumenthal's Discount Bridal on 22nd Street in Lombard. Rocco and I have purchased it. It's now called Bliss Bridals and will feature high end, designer gowns including the full Bellatoni line and my own custom designs under the 'Hannah by Bellatoni' label."

Leah was stunned. When did all this happen? She'd obviously missed some important family events over the last few weeks.

Hannah gestured toward the mystery woman with the tape measure around her neck and she came forward smiling brightly. "Maria Louisa, one of Rocco's *many* cousins, is in charge of alterations for the dress you choose and will have it ready before we leave for St. Lucia on Friday."

"Soon she'll be *your* cousin, too, you know," Rocco teased from her cellphone speaker.

Rocco and Hannah were engaged and in business together? Leah's heart sank. She'd been so self-absorbed in her own misery she was completely in the dark.

Hannah took her hands and squeezed them gently. "It's all right, Leah. You've been distracted the past couple of weeks. Rocco proposed toward the end of Luke and Abbey's wedding. A lot's happened that you've missed, but it's a story for another time, okay? Today is all about *you*."

Leah sighed, and tears pricked at her eyes. She'd already left the wedding by then and missed Rocco's proposal. Hannah and Rocco's purchase of Blumenthal's must have been in the works for some time, but she'd also missed that important development.

"Babe, Rocco's proposal is on the wedding DVD, so you can watch it. I'm so sorry, since I'm the reason you left early and missed it," Heath offered apologetically.

Leah wiped away a stray tear. She stood tall, with a renewed sense of excitement. She couldn't undo what had already happened, but she could embrace *now*. Everyone had gone to great lengths for her, and she would show her appreciation and gratitude by being joyful and in the moment.

"You're right. But after I select my dress and accessories, Hannah, promise you'll fill me in on everything that's happened." Leah wanted to know every detail she'd missed and vowed to be present from now on.

"You've got a deal." Hannah smiled and gestured to the dress racks. Leah turned to the ladies waiting impatiently with their Yes/No paddles and drinks in their hands. They seemed ready to get the wedding dress party started.

She handed Hannah her phone so she could get her hands on the exquisite dresses she had to choose from. Carefully, she examined each one on its hanger. Each was lovely in its own way. She stopped dead in her tracks when her eyes landed on the dream dress she'd seen online.

She sobbed in disbelief and awe. How could they have known? She hadn't told anyone about the dress she'd fallen in love with. It had dainty lace-capped sleeves with crystal decorated illusion mesh from the neck to the bust line. The bodice was decorated in a geometrically crisscrossing crystal and beaded pattern that extended over the hips to mid-thigh. From mid-thigh the dress was decorated in delicate crystal and beaded patterns with an airy, flowing cathedral train. She couldn't believe it was hers if she wanted it.

"Babe? Do I need to come downstairs? Are you all right?" The concern in Heath's voice caused her to sob harder. Hannah put an arm around her, seemingly trying to comfort her but not appearing concerned. She understood women got emotional shopping for their wedding gown.

"This … this is my dream dress. How did you know?" Her mother brought tissues and helped her wipe her face. "Thanks, Mom. I'm okay, just overwhelmed."

"We didn't," Heath and Hannah replied in unison.

"Heath and I spoke with Enzo and Paulo

Bellatoni about you. They sent dresses they thought you would like based on what we told them and pictures we sent them. They had your measurements from when they made your bridesmaid dress for Abbey and Luke's wedding and adjusted for a little pregnancy weight," Hannah informed her and placed a comforting hand on her shoulder.

"Is that all right? Are *you* all right?" Heath pressed.

Leah turned to the ladies seated near her, friends and family who meant the world to her. She did her best to ignore the cameraman capturing every moment that would air for who knew how many to see.

She smiled and nodded, knowing Heath couldn't see her, but he'd see when the episode aired. "I'm more than all right. I'm perfect. All of this, our family, our friends ... is perfect."

****

Heath had just finished shaving after an invigorating shower in his villa's garden shower when he thought he heard someone knocking on his door. He didn't have his hearing aids in so he couldn't be sure. He wiped his face with a damp towel, pleased he hadn't nicked himself as he examined his reflection in the mirror. That wouldn't do on his wedding day.

He'd slept soundly the last few nights. Although his sleeping pills were the lowest dosage available they were too strong, leaving him groggy and out of it the following morning, though nightmare-free. Three nights ago, he'd taken a half dose in addition to listening to the soothing nature sounds of an amazing 3D holographic sound app, and to his relief, he'd been able to sleep well without nightmares and felt refreshed in the morning. If only he'd thought of trying that sooner. *Better late than never. Progress.*

He turned his head when he thought he heard knocking again. He rushed to the door, the local stone tiled floor cool under his bare feet, a fluffy Providence St. Lucia towel wrapped around his waist.

He opened the door to find Rocco standing there dressed for his and Leah's wedding day, in light colored linen slacks and a crisp white dress shirt with the sleeves rolled halfway up his forearms. Heath didn't panic. He knew he had plenty of time to get ready for his wedding. Rocco didn't appear upset so he was most likely there to provide an update on the day's arrangements.

Before Rocco spoke, Heath signed he didn't have his hearing aids in and stepped aside so Rocco could enter. He headed to the villa's bedroom to get his hearing aids with Rocco following closely behind.

Grabbing them from the top of mahogany dresser and slipping them into place, he turned to Rocco with a smile on his face, eager for news.

"Kitchen staff is ready to go. Everyone's going to be pleased regardless of what they choose from the buffet. The outdoor deck is set up for anyone who wants to eat outside rather than in the Event Center," Rocco assured him.

He and Leah had wanted to give their guests the option of where they enjoyed their reception meal. Nodding, he tossed his towel aside and slipped into white boxer briefs. Rocco made himself comfortable in one of the room's brightly colored cushioned chairs.

"And outside?" He unzipped the black garment bag that held his light grey suit. The suit he'd wear to marry the love of his life. He shook his head, still unable to fully believe this was happening.

"Hannah's got it covered and ready. Just like you wanted. A platform on the sand for the guest chairs, the wood canopy area up front where you'll get married, and an extra wide aisle from the resort, with the guest chairs on either side leading to the canopy area. Everything's decorated with island flowers. And Plan B is set up in the Event Center in case it rains." Rocco glanced out one of the bedroom windows and smiled.

From what Heath could see looking outside himself, it was clear and mostly sunny. Right now, at least. He hoped the weather held until after the ceremony, but a Plan B was necessary.

Dressed except for his jacket, he pocketed the small folding tactical knife he always carried with him. The cool metal felt comforting in his hand.

Rocco checked his watch and stood. "We still have a few minutes, but get everything you need so you're not late."

Grabbing his jacket, he and Rocco made their way to the main living space of the villa. Rocco headed to the veranda. Heath retrieved a single white rose from the kitchenette's refrigerator and joined Rocco outside.

The view was nothing short of spectacular. Paradise. They were surrounded by lush rain forest and the sound of waves gently crashing against the shore of the resort's private, pristine Caribbean beach. He inhaled the warm tropical air and felt a sense of calm he hadn't felt in a long time. Too long.

"How the fuck did we get here?"

Rocco chuckled. "We flew, remember?"

Heath shook his head, reveling in the clear blue majestic ocean before him. "Asshole. *Stronzo.* Did you ever think when we were in the shit, we'd end up here?" He knew *he* didn't. Marrying Leah and becoming a father weren't in the realm of possibility after Sangin. Hell, even before then if he were being honest.

"Hell no. Even before Afghanistan I never imaged anything like this could be possible." Rocco reached into his pants pocket and handed Heath a small black velvet pouch. "You can't get married without these."

He held the pouch in his hand. Their rings felt substantial, solid, and significant. He couldn't wait until Leah was legally his.

He pocketed the rings and checked his watch. It was time to go. "You sure you and Hannah don't want to make this a double wedding? Everything's already set up." He suspected he knew Rocco's answer, but he also knew Rocco was as anxious to marry his girl as Heath was to marry his.

Rocco sighed and shook his head regretfully. "I would love that, but her gown is almost ready. The first in Hannah's line and with everything we and the Bellatonis have planned—it's only three more weeks. Hannah deserves her special day."

Heath clapped Rocco on the shoulder. "So do you, brother."

The Italian's smile lit up his face. "Hell yeah, I do. But right now, we've got to get *you* married. Let's go. *Andiamo.*"

He was wholeheartedly on board with that idea. Following Rocco out of his villa, they strode with determination toward the resort's main entrance. Hannah was waiting for them dressed in a pretty pink flowered dress holding his red rose boutonniere, with a bright smile on her face.

She made quick work pinning it on his lapel and stood back, looking him over. Seemingly pleased with his appearance, she nodded. "Perfect." She turned to Rocco with a tender smile. "Three more weeks and it'll be us."

He embraced his fiancée with such gentle care Heath's eyes stung. The event planner and the Italian had also found their perfect. He and Rocco were two lucky fuckers all right.

"*Stasera sei tutta mia,*" Rocco said with a gleam in his eyes. Hannah promptly blushed and teasingly pushed him away. Heath didn't have to know Italian to know whatever Rocco said had something to do with sex.

He chuckled at the pair. "Save it for later. I'm about to get married."

"Sorry, brother." After a quick man hug and a kiss on Hannah's cheek, Rocco took his place on the right side of the aisle.

"It's time for you to take your place up front." Hannah kissed his cheek and stepped aside.

Heath took a deep breath and gazed at the white rose in his hand. A symbol of his late mother. He'd felt her presence since they'd arrived at the resort and felt it still. Loving and comforting, just like when she'd been alive. She'd loved Leah like her own, and he knew deep in his heart and soul she approved of their union.

With an overwhelming sense of gratitude and a warm island breeze behind him, Heath headed toward his place up front, doing his best not to run in order to speed things along. Everyone who meant anything to him were seated, from members of his former Marine unit, including his Sergeant Major and Gunnery Sergeant, to his dearest friends and family. Not able to choose one as "the best", he and Leah had agreed to forgo a traditional bridal party.

When he reached his father in the front row, he placed the white rose on the empty chair beside him. With a warm smile on his face and tears in his eyes, his father nodded. Heath knew today was difficult for him, but his father was working hard to deal with his issues, too.

"I'm proud of you, son," his father whispered.

Heath winked at his father and took his place to the right of the officiant, who was dressed in a black suit and white collar. When everyone stood, his heart thundered in his chest. This was it, at long last. In a few minutes his life would be complete. He'd survived against nearly impossible odds in Sangin, and Leah and their unborn child were his prize.

Leah looked like a dream in her designer Bellatoni gown. What a stroke of luck or fate it had been selected as an option for her to choose from. When her father placed her delicate hand in his, Heath thought his heart would burst out of his chest it was so full.

Not able to wait, he kissed the love of his life, not caring it wasn't that point in the proceedings yet. He couldn't wait. He needed a taste of her.

The officiant cleared his throat rather loudly, and Leah pulled away, giggling along with their guests.

"Go, Marine," someone shouted, and everyone full out laughed.

"Are you two ready to get started?" their officiant asked, with a smile on his face.

"Yes, sorry," Leah replied, looking so incredibly beautiful Heath's eyes stung.

Hold on just a few more minutes.

With the sound of waves gently crashing to the shore in the background and the soft breeze carrying the scent of the flowers that decorated their space, the officiant began the ceremony.

"The bride and groom wanted to keep things short and sweet, so let us begin. Family and friends, we have been invited here today to share with Heath and Leah a very important moment in their lives. In the many years they have known each other, their love and understanding of each other has grown and matured, and now they have decided to live the rest of their lives together as husband

and wife."

Leah smiled at him with tears streaming down her lovely cheeks. The officiant paused as Heath quickly wiped them away and some of his own. "It's okay, babe."

She nodded and squeezed his hands.

"Matrimony is commended to be honorable among all men and women; and therefore, is not to be entered into unadvisedly or lightly, but reverently, discreetly, advisedly and solemnly," the officiant continued. "May I have the rings please?"

Heath retrieved the velvet ring pouch from his pocket and handed it to the officiant. They were close, just their simple vows, ring exchange, and Leah was his for good.

"Leah, please state your intentions."

"I, Leah, take you, Heath, to be my husband, my partner in life, and my one true love. I will cherish our union and love you more each day than I did the day before. I will trust you and respect you, laugh with you and cry with you, loving you faithfully through good times and bad, regardless of the obstacles we may face together. I give you my hand, my heart, and my love, from this day forward for as long as we both shall live."

The officiant handed Leah his wedding ring. Leah's hand shook slightly as she slipped it on his ring ringer. "With this ring, I thee wed."

"Oorah," all the Marines shouted.

"Heath, please state your intentions."

There was so much he wanted to say, and would say eventually, but today he'd settle for his vows. He held on tightly to her hands. "I, Heath, take you, Leah, to be my friend, my lover, the mother of my children, and my wife. I will be yours in times of plenty and in times of want, in times of sickness and in times of health, in times of joy and in times of sorrow, in times of failure and in times of triumph. I promise to cherish and respect you, to care for and protect you, to comfort and encourage you, and stay with you, for all eternity. I give you my hand, my heart, and my love, from this day forward for as long as we both shall live."

The officiant gave Heath Leah's engagement ring and matching wedding band. Tears ran down his face as he slipped her rings on. "With these rings, I thee wed." He kissed her knuckles tenderly and wiped more tears from her cheeks.

When all the Marines in attendance shouted "Oorah" again, Heath didn't hesitate and claimed his wife's lips, unconcerned with what the officiant had left to say. Leah was now his, and that's all that mattered. He ended their much too brief kiss when he felt his cock twitch in his suit pants. *That* would have to wait until later.

Until they were in their five-bedroom private villa a short walk from the main resort. He intended on christening each bedroom and spending quality naked time in the villa's infinity pool with his bride.

They both turned to face their guests and were greeted with cheers, whistles, and applause. Heath raised their joined hands in victory … and thunder clapped.

"Oh shit!" Not wanting to risk Leah getting her gown wet, he whisked her back up the aisle to a shower of rose petals thrown by their guests. Everyone hustled to the resort's entrance, and just as he and Leah stepped inside the entrance, it began to rain.

Rocco had told him Italians considered rain on your wedding day to be good luck. It symbolized cleansing and fertility. Since Leah was carrying their child, they were halfway there already. They'd gotten through the ceremony before the rain had started. He considered it a win.

Heath claimed his bride's lips while their guests

came in from the rain and began heading to the Event Center for dinner. "Ready to get this party started, Mrs. Jackson?"

Leah's eyes widened. "Mrs. Jackson. I like the sound of that. Yes, let's do that … and then on to what happens next," she replied sweetly with a gleam in her eyes.

"You got it, babe." He escorted his bride to dinner feeling optimistic and joyful. Looking forward to what happened next after their wedding festivities, but also eager for what lay ahead beyond their stay in paradise.

- **Epilogue**

About six months later

Heath was thankful for Chicago's snow removal expertise as Luke sped them westward on I-290 from Cobras' HQ to Edward-Elmhurst Hospital. The streets were well plowed and salted after a storm dumped over six inches of snow three days before. It was mid-March, and even though they were heading into spring with temperatures normally in the low to mid-forties, he knew from experience they could still be surprised with significant snowfall.

He shook his head listening to Luke laugh while they passed all the cars around them following their police escort out of Chicago. When he'd received the call from his mother-in-law during lunch informing him Leah had gone into labor a week early, he'd nearly panicked. He'd ridden the Metra train to the office and was at the mercy of their schedule.

Fortunately, Luke had driven in and had immediately volunteered to bring him to Leah and his anxious-to-be-born daughter, Faith. On a whim Luke had called 911 and within moments a Chicago police squad car was leading the way to the hospital, sirens blaring.

Leah was keeping the middle name she'd chosen for their little girl a secret from everyone until she was born. It seemed he'd find out soon enough.

"Is this some cool action movie shit or what," Luke commented loudly so he could be heard over the sirens.

Heath rolled his eyes. "This is nothing. I've been in combat, asshole." He suppressed a grin, not wanting to admit that in the *civilian* world a police escort down a busy Chicago highway was indeed pretty cool. There were a few scattered icy spots along their route though. "Be careful. The last thing we need is to get into an accident on the way."

"No worries, big brother. My Range Rover Sport will get us to the hospital safely. Now back to our conversation before little Faith surprised us a week early," Luke said, apparently trying to distract him during their trek to the hospital.

Heath groaned. *Not this again.* "Luke, you can't marry off my daughter to your unborn son." Abbey was pregnant with a boy and was due in about five weeks, and his sister Sylvia was due around the same time. Their family was experiencing a baby boom.

Luke frowned, keeping his eyes on the road and the police car in front of him. "Why not? Because Ethan will be a few weeks younger than Faith? You're ten years older than Leah, and it hasn't made any difference."

"It's not the age difference, idiot. I want my daughter to choose her own husband, and you should want Ethan to choose his own wife. We shouldn't be trying to *force* them together." He was about to point out Jake wasn't pushing his three-month-old Justin on Faith but remembered they were first cousins. They weren't having *that* conversation.

Luke sighed again and shrugged. "You're right, but if they decide they want to be together somewhere down the line you won't stand in the way, right?"

Why was Luke so insistent? It would be years before any of this mattered. "If it's what they both truly want, then I won't stand in the way," he conceded.

Luke smiled happily, seemingly pleased with Heath's response. "Great! If they marry, we'll be related. Actual family. That'd be awesome, wouldn't it?"

He'd considered Luke family since they met

when they were little boys. Hell, Luke had only been two when they met. Now Heath felt like an ass. After losing his parents when he was ten and with his Uncle Darren's pancreatic cancer diagnosis, it wasn't surprising Luke's concern was about family. He should have known why Luke hoped their kids would end up together.

Heath's heart thundered in his chest as they followed the squad car to the east entrance of the hospital parking lot.

I'm coming, Leah! Hang in there just a little longer.

"It'd be fucking amazing," Heath said as they came to a stop. "Family Birthing Center's on the third floor."

In his rush to get to Leah, Heath wasn't paying attention and slipped and fell on some ice a few feet in front of the hospital entrance doors. *Fuck!* On his hands and knees doing his best to calm down, he felt himself being pulled up by the two Chicago police officers that had escorted them to the hospital.

"Careful now. Your wife's counting on you to be in one piece," the young officer with Allinson on his name badge said.

"Good luck," the older, probably more experienced officer with Warner on his name badge said.

"Thank you. For everything." Heath cautiously walked the rest of the way until he was safely inside the hospital.

After what seemed like an eternity, the elevator doors dinged and slid open to the third floor. He exited right and ran down the hallway to the Family Birthing Center. His stomach knotted when he saw Leah's mother outside what must be their private birthing suite. Was something wrong? He didn't think he'd survive if anything happened to Leah or Faith.

His mother-in-law smiled tightly when he reached her and hugged him. He braced himself for the worst. "Luke texted me you were on your way up. She's doing great, but she won't take any nitrous oxide for the pain. You made it just in time. Faith's head just crowned."

The hospital used nitrous oxide for labor pain and anxiety. It was deemed safe for both mommy and baby and exited their systems quickly. Why was Leah refusing to use it?

"Where's my husband? Heath!" Leah's cries for him nearly had him in tears, her sobs hurting his soul.

Leah's mother patted him on the shoulder. "Go on in there. She needs you. I'll call everyone and let them know she's in labor."

Too emotional to respond, he nodded and went to help his wife. Inside their birthing suite he found Leah moaning, her face and hair damp with sweat with her legs in stirrups and their doctor in scrubs at the foot of the bed. A delivery nurse by his side. He tore out of his coat, ripped off his gloves, and tossed them aside.

Leah looked at him, sobbing with pain etched on her beautiful face, and he felt like shit. He'd done this to her. Caused her this pain. He was beside her in an instant, holding her hand and kissed her damp forehead. "Luke got me here with a police escort," he blurted out, unsure of what to say to comfort his wife. *She doesn't care about that, you idiot.*

To his surprise, even in the midst of painful labor, she laughed. Then moaned in pain. "I'll thank him later for bringing you to me. Please put the top hat on. It's on the chair."

She'd brought the top hat? God, he loved this woman. The top hat sat proudly, like a beacon, on the chair in the corner that could also be used during labor.

He quickly put it on and retuned to Leah's side.

"Leah, one more big push and you'll be a mommy," the doctor announced behind his surgical mask.

She sobbed and shook her head. "It hurts. I can't."

He stopped short of nagging her about the nitrous oxide and looked into her pained, fearful face. "Yes, you can, babe. Because you're amazing and me and Faith are so lucky to have you. And I know you want to kill me right now because I'm the reason you're in so much pain, but I can't wait to have more kids with you. I love you so much."

For some reason, she looked stunned. Didn't she know by now how much she meant to him?

"I love you, too. I always have. But let's wait a little while before we have another one." She grimaced as another contraction hit, and she squeezed his hand. Hard.

"Now, Leah. One final push," the doctor demanded.

"You can do this, dear," the labor nurse encouraged.

The love of his life bore down with a scream and brought their little girl into the world right before his eyes. She collapsed back on the hospital bed exhausted but with a contented smile on her face. "I did it," she whispered.

"You sure did. You were amazing, babe." He kissed her smiling lips and held her close while the doctor and nurse tended to their wailing little girl and her now weary mother. "She's got quite a set of lungs on her, huh?"

"I bet you'd be able to hear her without your hearing aids in," Leah teased. He didn't doubt it, and that had been a concern. Their townhouse was now equipped with baby monitors throughout both floors and the basement, turned up to full volume.

A short while later the labor nurse brought over a still wailing, squirming pink bundle with dark blonde hair and gently placed her in his shaking arms. Nervous as hell, he accepted his baby girl and with awe and wonder, and rocked her tiny form, hoping to calm her down.

He didn't know what to expect, but was surprised she was so light. So delicate. So incredibly perfect. Precious. When she opened her stunning green eyes and looked at him for the first time, he was utterly lost and overwhelmed, and tears streamed down his face.

"Hey there, angel, no need to cry. Mommy and Daddy are right here. We'll take good care of you," he whispered to his newborn daughter.

Leah leaned over slightly in her bed so she could stroke their daughter's tearstained cheeks. "Everything will be all right, Faith Heather," she sweetly assured their little girl.

His eyes widened, and he continued gently rocking Faith as she settled down. "Heather? Like *my* name?" He placed their now cooing baby in Leah's outstretched arms.

"Exactly like your name. Oh Heath, she's so beautiful. She's got your dark blonde hair and your family's green eyes."

He knew that for the rest of his life he'd never forget the indescribably beautiful picture his wife holding their daughter made. His heart was full, his life complete. And to think he'd denied his feelings for Leah for so many years, feeling unworthy, insecure and guilty. What a fool he'd been. With the help and encouragement of his family and counselor he had everything he could have ever hoped for.

"Congratulations, you two. Faith Heather weighed in at 7.34 pounds and is 19.3 inches long. It's the hospital's quiet time now for visitors, so we'll leave the three of alone. If you need anything just press the call button on your bed's remote control," the doctor instructed them, and he and the nurse slipped out of the room.

Heath touched his little girl's tiny hand, and she wrapped it around his finger. Her powerful little grip brought tears to his eyes.

"I want to hold on to your daddy all the time, too," Lead admitted to Faith. "He's an amazing man. He, your great- and great-great-grandpas are honorable Marines. So when you're a big girl if you're called to serve, I suggest getting your college degree first and then requesting OCS, Officer Candidacy School. But you don't have to worry about that now. If and when the time comes you can talk with Daddy and Uncle Rocco about what's best," she whispered to their now sleeping child.

His heart swelled with gratitude for his wife. He'd wait a few more minutes before sharing the happy news with their waiting family members.

Right now, he was more than content to privately revel in their kind of perfect just a little while longer.

The End

www.daniavoss.com

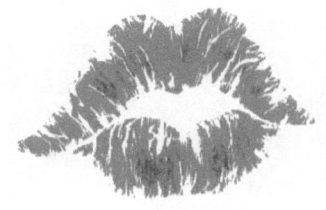

EVERNIGHT PUBLISHING ®

www.evernightpublishing.com

www.ingramcontent.com/pod-product-compliance
Lightning Source LLC
Chambersburg PA
CBHW022015170626
46808CB00001B/426